Body of Evidence

An Ed Lazenby Mystery

Charles Ray

North Potomac, MD

This book is a work of fiction. Names, incidents, and descriptions are the products of the author's imagination, and any similarity to and incident, organization, or person (living or dead) is purely coincidental.

Cover design by the author using CoverGenie.Pro and photo by the author.

Printed in the United States of America.

ISBN: 0692128344
ISBN-13: 978-0692128343

DEDICATION

To the valiant men and women of the Maine State Police. I hope that my portrayal of you is accurate, but know that your service to your communities is not unappreciated..

CHAPTER 1

Edward Lazenby, Ed to his close friends, of which there were few, was an unhappy camper. In fact, since he'd turned eleven over sixty years in his dimly-remembered past, and his mother had convinced (ordered) him to join the local Boy Scout troop so that he could get out of his bedroom where he could usually be found with his nose in a book and get some fresh air and learn to be a 'normal' boy, he had *hated* camping.

The experience had been traumatic. There were bugs that got into your food and your sleeping bag, and kept you awake at night with their incessant buzzing and chirping, the fear of snakes slithering into your tent while you slept, and the smell of ten to twelve other boys tramping around the woods without bathing for two to three days at a time.

Out of respect for his mother, he'd stuck it out until he graduated from high school, but when he left home, headed for college, he'd trashed the contact information his troop leader had given him for the Eagle Scout troop near Wiley College where he'd enrolled as a freshman.

His next unpleasant experience with the outdoors had come when he enlisted in the army. Basic training, with the obligatory bivouac, and wouldn't you know, it rained the entire time, and it took him four days to get all the mud out of the crevices of his body and his tightly curled hair, was even worse than the scouts had been. Fortunately, his placement test scores were off the charts, so he'd been selected for special training as an intelligence analyst, and during that training had shown facility with numbers, so he'd eventually been trained as a systems analyst.

During his twenty years in the army, he'd only ever slept in a tent during basic training. The machines he was required to use required a climate-controlled environment, and as their operator, he insisted on bunking close to them, which meant that whenever he worked with a field unit, he slept in his air-conditioned trailer.

So, he wondered, and not for the first time, why in the blue blazes am I here on this rickety ferry boat—something else he wasn't particularly fond of because boats had a disturbing tendency to sink—headed for some remote place in the wilds to spend the next seven days 'experiencing' nature?

What he'd experienced of it since leaving the dock at Bar Harbor didn't impress him much. Sure, he thought, the views of the ocean, the town nestled in the hills along the shore, and the abundance of bird life was interesting, but he could have stayed at home and watched it on the *National Geographic* channel and not have to deal with the pack of people on the swaying boat, or the constant chatter from Rose Wertheim, one of his few friends, as she pointed out interesting—to her—sights, or related the history of the area to Ernesto Cardoza, his across-the-street neighbor and best friend at Potomac Valley Community, or PVC for short, the retirement in which they all lived. Rose's older sister, Violet, looked as unimpressed with their surroundings as Ed felt. She stood at the rail, her back half turned to Ernesto and her sister, her face set in its usual scowl, staring out at the dark blue ocean to their east.

He debated walking over and talking to her, and then thought he'd just leave her to whatever she was thinking. In his mood, he would only aggravate her, and possibly initiate one of her criticism sessions.

He was just turning back to take in the view when Rose and Ernesto moved his way. He didn't feel like engaging in one of Rose's long-winded conversations, always one-sided with her doing most of the talking, but there was no where to go on the sardine can of a boat they were on. He took a deep breath and turned to face them.

"Such a beautiful view, don't you think, Ed?" Rose said in her gushy tone.

"It's okay," he responded.

"Just okay? Where are your eyes. Look at that beautiful ocean, that beautiful sky, and oh, the scenery along the coast is to die for. Isn't that right, Ernesto?"

"Of course, it is, Rose," Ernesto said, shooting Ed a glare. "Ed's just pissed because he's missing his Saturday golf game."

"You can play golf anytime, Ed." Rose put her hands on her hips, swaying with the motion of the boat. "It's not often you get the chance to experience such beauty *and* get fit at the same time."

She was referring to the package tour she'd signed the four of them up for. Wilmot's Wilderness Adventures, a newly-established travel agency offering nontraditional tours, was taking the four of them and eight other couples on what they billed as a 'Wilderness retreat that will build your survival skills, increase your knowledge of nature, and lift your spirits.' So far, Ed thought, they'd done nothing for his spirit, and their guide, Jason Wilmot, part-owner of the company with his older brother, Leonard, didn't talk much, and looked like he'd be more at home in a gym than in the outdoors. The man's shoulder and chest muscles threatened to burst out of his red and black flannel shirt. Ed suspected t hat he had a book hidden in his backpack which he consulted before giving one of his infrequent nature lectures, something he'd done during the two-day bus ride from Washington, DC to Bar Harbor, Maine. He tried not to think about the survival skills part of the offering. As a boy scout, he'd taken most of the first year after signing up to learn how to make a fire by rubbing two sticks together. Mostly what he got from that was blisters and sore knees from crouching so long trying to coax a few sparks from the twigs that were supposed to start a campfire. Still, Rose and Ernesto counted as his two best friends; Violet was just a friend, or as he'd heard the younger members of PVC's staff say, a frenemy, so he didn't want to upset them.

"It's okay," he said. "It's just a bit chilly for me."

A bit chilly was an understatement. Maine's weather in June was like mid-March in DC, chilly, with too much moisture in the air, making it feel colder than it actually was, and here on the coast, the wind never seemed to stop blowing.

"Oh, poo, Ed Lazenby," Rose said. "You've played golf in weather a lot colder than this."

She had him there. How do you explain that it's different when you're doing something you enjoy? You don't.

"It's the boat," he said. "I've always hated boats. That's why I joined the army after college, you know. I had a couple of classmates; one joined the marines and the other the navy, and they both tried to get me to go along, but the idea of spending so much time surrounded by that much water is not at all appealing. I'll be better once we're back on dry land."

He looked around as he spoke. 'Dry land,' indeed. There was so much moisture in the northeast New

England air you could feel it on your skin, and your clothes felt damp and soggy.

Rose, though, didn't react to the frown, or the obvious sarcasm in his voice. Rose was like that, always looking for the bright side of things.

"Well, okay then," she said. "We'll hold you to that. Now, come on Ernesto, let's see what old grumpy Violet's up to."

Charles Ray

CHAPTER 2

As much as he liked the two of them, Ed was happy to see them go. He decided to move to another part of the boat just in case Rose remembered something else she wanted to say to him.

He began making his way to the rear, he reminded himself to think, 'stern,' of the ferry, apologizing to two couples, standing at the rail looking at the scenery, that he had to squeeze past. They were so engrossed in the sights, though, that they didn't even acknowledge his apologies.

Finally, he found a place where there was no one else that he would have to interact with, a rectangular space hemmed in by wooden crates stacked two-high at the very rear of the ferry. He leaned on the rail and stared absently at the water that seemed to be moving past the hull of the craft, and the irregular v-shaped wake that it left behind. The antics of the gulls, as they engaged in mid-air duels over the debris thrown over the rails of the ferry, and churned about by the wake, were interesting to watch, and for a moment, alone there, with just the squawking of the warring gulls, the splash of the ocean against the hull, and the hum of the engines for company, he almost felt at ease.

Then, he heard voices.

At first, the conversation was unintelligible. But, as Ed moved closer to the stack of crates on his left he began to make out what was being said.

"It was a mistake letting you talk me into coming on this trip," a woman's voice said.

It was answered by a man's voice, and Ed could hear the frustration and anger. "We need to make a new start, babe," the male voice said. "I figured this would be a good way to get that start. Come on, give it a chance, you'll love it."

"Love, hah! That's a funny word for *you* to be using."

"What the hell is that supposed to mean?"

"You know what it means, you know very well what it means. I know about your other women."

"Aw, babe, gimme a break. So, I screwed up one time. I'm sorry. This is my way of making that right. Forgive me?"

"I don't know, I just don't know. You shredded our marriage vows when you went to a motel with that bimbo."

"I know that, and I'm so, so sorry. I was drunk. That's a lame excuse, but I swear it's the truth, and I also promise you it'll never happen again."

"I don't know if I can."

"You got all the time in the world. Things are gonna get put right this trip, I promise you that." Now Ed heard a little hardness in the man's tone that didn't seem to match his words.

"Okay, I'll give it a try, but I'm not making any promises. I'm still hurt and angry. Why, though, does it have to be camping? You know how I hate the outdoors; the insects and things creep me out."

"You're gonna love it, babe. I promise you."

Ed was beginning to feel uncomfortable, eavesdropping on a private spat between spouses. He could sympathize with the wife, first for her husband cheating on her, and secondly, bringing her on a trip which she clearly was not up for. On the other hand, he didn't know the whole story. She had a whiny kind of voice; maybe she was constantly nagging him. Maybe she spent too much on clothes and jewelry.

The best thing for him to do was move away and wipe the memory of the overheard conversation from his mind.

Like that was even possible. Ed was, unfortunately, saddled with a mind that absorbed and retained almost everything he heard or saw. Not that he had an eidetic memory, that ability commonly incorrectly called a photographic memory, but pretty darn close. The conversation would keep floating around just at the edge of his consciousness for days before it was overwritten by something new.

He backed slowly away from the crates so as to make no noise. No sense the couple, whoever they were, knowing an old man had been snooping.

Might as well go back and listen to Rose. I'm gonna be stuck with her for days, anyway, so it'll probably bother me less if I get an overdose of it before we even arrive at the camp site.

Charles Ray

CHAPTER 3

He got lucky. Rose only bothered him a couple of times, but she was so busy educating Ernesto she basically ignored him for most of the rest of the journey. Violet, for her part, communicated in grunts once of twice when he tried, out of politeness, to engage her in conversation.

Her face seemed frozen in a scowl until the ferry's horn sounded and looking forward, they saw they were approaching a low wooden pier jutting out into the surf.

Violet, upon seeing the pier, smiled for the first time since leaving home.

"At last," she said. "Good old solid ground."

She said it in a low murmur, but Ed was standing near and overheard.

"I see you like boats about as much as I do," he said. "Which is not at all."

"Hmph, if God had meant for us to spend time on water, he would've given us fins and gills. Besides, I hate that constant swaying and bouncing up and down. It's like a slow-motion earthquake."

Ed laughed. "I never thought of it like that before, but you're right, and who the heck wants to spend hours or days in an earthquake."

"Well," Violet said. "We're here now. Let's get our bags and get off this thing before they turn around and start back and we're stuck on it."

Ed knew that would never happen, and he knew Violet knew it as well. It was her attempt at humor. Not bad for humorless Violet. Ed laughed again.

His good humor disappeared, though, when their tour guide appeared in front of him. Jason Wilmot stopped and faced Ed, his muscular arms on his narrow hips, his massive chest expanded to its fullest, and a self-satisfied smirk on his face.

"Mr. Lazenby, is it?" When Ed nodded, he said, "I pride myself on knowing each of my clients. I also *know* them, and you, Mr. Lazenby, are, I believe, not too happy about being here."

Despite himself, Ed was impressed for all of two seconds. Then, he realized that he'd been scowling since they boarded the bus in front of the community building at PVC.

Wilmot, though, turned away from him and fixed his steely gaze on Violet, who stood a step behind Ed.

"And, you," he said. "Ms. Violet Wertheim, are also not a happy camper."

Violet snorted.

"That's okay," he went on, as if nothing untoward had just happened. "Before this trip is over, the both of you will be devotees of the outdoors."

"I seriously doubt that," Violet said.

Ed nodded his agreement.

Wilmot laughed. "So, that's the way it's gonna be, eh? Okay, I'll make you two a deal. If you're not lovin' it half way through the coming week, I'll refund your entire fee. If you *are* lovin' it, though, the two of you will do a promo commercial for us. How's that for a deal, eh?"

Violet immediately said, yes. Ed thought about it for a few seconds. Of course, he knew his mind wouldn't change, but, he thought, what if it did? Do I really want to look stupid standing in front of a camera telling people how wonderful this whole mess is? Then, he decided, what the hell. It would be a free vacation, because hell would be an ice lake before he ever liked camping.

"You got yourself a deal," he said.

"Good, now let's put our bags in the vans and get to the camp site so we can get introduced and start cooking supper."

Along with Wilmot and twelve others; four couples along with Ed and his three friends; they piled into two large Econoline vans with their luggage. The drivers, two locals who responded to their 'hellos' with nods and taciturn looks, drove them along a winding, tree-lined road away from the docks and in a southeasterly direction along the rocky coast of the island.

Peter Pace and Daryl Drum, from the Adams-Morgan area of the District of Columbia, a couple who had taken advantage of Massachusetts' enlightened attitude toward the institution of marriage and legalized their union in that state in 2004, a week after the state became the first in the U.S. to issue marriage licenses to same-sex couples. Fortunately, Wilmot, who seemed to avoid conversation with the two men as much as possible, had gone with the other three couples in the other van, which suited Ed just fine.

The others had introduced themselves on the ferry; Tom and Janet Evans from Fairfax City, Virginia; George and Lilian Lake from Germantown, Maryland; and Harry and Gertrude Pope from Bethesda. Ed acknowledged them, gave his name, and wandered off to gaze at the rapidly receding shoreline, so he'd missed the obligatory biographic information that inevitably comes out when people are first introduced. Rose, on the other hand, had, while still regaling Ernesto with her knowledge of the region, managed to 'get the dope', as she was fond of saying, on everyone.

And, as usual, she couldn't resist letting Ed and Ernesto know it.

"So, Peter," she said. "You're a computer game designer. That sounds so interesting. You must be awful smart to do such work."

Pace beamed at Rose's flattery. Ed put a hand over his mouth and coughed to keep from laughing aloud.

"I've always been interested in computer games," Pace said. "So, it seemed a natural career for me."

Drum put an arm around his partner's shoulder. "Pete just launched a game similar to *Tetris*, but with more challenges. It's gonna take the game world by storm."

Pace blushed and punched Drum's shoulder. "Oh, it's not all that."

"I bet it is," Rose said. "When you're all rich and famous, please don't forget you know a plain, common old lady, will you?"

"I don't think I could ever forget you, Rose."

Ed could understand that sentiment. Rose could be a bit much at times, but she was such a good-hearted person, anyone who met her liked her. Now, Violet was an entirely different matter. She took a lot of getting used to. The milk of human kindness was in her, but she kept it under a thick layer of skepticism. That skepticism came out at that moment.

"That's for sure," she said. "My nosy kid sister gets her nose so deep into your business, you couldn't forget her if you tried."

"I didn't mean it like that," Pace said, holding his hand up in protest. "I meant because she's such a nice person."

Ed saw the flicker of a smile quickly come and go on Violet's face and figured out what she was up to. She was bored, and this was her way of amusing herself. On the one hand, he could sympathize with her. The trip, thus far, had been a tad boring, but on the other, he felt she needed to be brought down a peg or two.

"Oh, ignore Violet," he said. "She's just jealous because people like Rose more than they do her."

"Am not," Violet said.

"Are too," Ed shot back.

"Now, you two act your age," Rose said. "Do you want these nice young men to think we're all a bunch of doddering, senile old folks?"

"I am not doddering," Ernesto said. "I've never doddered in my life."

"And, I don't think I'm senile," Ed said. "I'm not so sure about Violet, though."

"Ed Lazenby, have you ever been short-sheeted?" Violet asked.

His eyes went wide. What did Violet know about an old army custom where someone folded your sheet in half and made your bed with it, so that when you got in, your feet were blocked halfway down the length of the bed.

"No, I have never been short-sheeted. Why do you ask?"

"Oh, just curious. We might be using sleeping bags, and I'm sure I can figure out how to short-sheet one. So, you'd better mind your mouth."

Pace and Drum were looking from one to the other of them like spectators at a fast-paced tennis match, their eyes wide, and their bodies tense.

Violet looked at them. Her lips turned up in a smile, and then she started laughing. Ed couldn't help himself. He, too, began laughing.

Pace and Drum looked confused.

"You should see the look on your faces," Ed said. "You look like you're worried we might come to blows."

That caused him to laugh harder.

"W-well, it was beginning to sound like it," Drum said.

Rose leaned across and patted his arm. "Ignore them," she said. "Ed and my sister are always doing dumb stuff like that. They were acting up, a bit over the top if you ask me, just to get a rise out of you boys."

When the realization hit that they'd been pranked, the two men began laughing. "Well, you certainly did that," Pace said. "You folks are gonna be fun to be around this week."

CHAPTER 4

Ed was surprised when the van drove onto a blacktop parking lot and parked in front of a small log cabin with a large green sign over the door that read, 'Wilmot's Wilderness Adventures, A Week You'll Never Forget' in gold letters. At the left of the letters was a painting of a fish jumping out of the water, and on the right a deer with a massive set of antlers.

There were four other log cabins to the left and four to the right, the same size, with green doors and large gold numbers on them, from 1 to 8, left to right.

"So," Ed said. "Looks like we don't have to sleep in tents. That's a relief."

"You should be used to sleeping in a tent," Violet said. "Weren't you in the army?"

"Yes, I was, but I only slept in a tent during basic training. I worked with computers and other sensitive devices, so the few times I had to go the field, I slept in an air-conditioned trailer. I hate tents, and I don't like sleeping on the ground."

"I hear that," Daryl Drum said.

"I think it would be fun," Rose said.

"I'm with Rose," Pace said, jabbing Drum's shoulder. "You guys are a bunch of wusses."

"Call me a wuss, or even something worse," Ed said. "I still prefer sleeping on a bed."

Their argument continued until they alighted from the van and came face to face with Jason Wilmot, who stood with his chest out and his hands on his hips, reminding Ed of one of his drill sergeants from basic training.

"Okay, people," Wilmot said. "Gather round, and I'll give you your cabin assignments."

Ed hung back near the van, put off by the way the rest crowded around Wilmot as if he was the candy man with a bag full of goodies. He never ceased to be amazed at the behavior of otherwise rational people once they became part of a group. The mob mind takes over and causes them to do things that, if alone, they would cringe at. Even Violet, normally a complete skeptic and the devil's advocate of most gatherings, seemed eager to see what Wilmot had to offer.

"Now, here's how this work," Wilmot said as soon as the murmuring and sounds of shuffling feet had died down. "In addition to being an adventure designed to help you get to know yourself better, this is a kind of couples' retreat. It'll help you put the juice back into your relationship."

Ed perked up. That was the first time he'd heard that little tidbit.

"That wasn't mentioned in your brochure," he said.

"We don't emphasize that part of the activity. It's just a plus. Call it a bonus."

"We're not having any of that touchy-feely nonsense, are we?" Violet asked.

Ed noticed that her skeptical expression had returned. Good, he thought. I prefer the old Violet.

"I'm not sure what you mean by touchy-feely," Wilmot said, glaring at Violet. "But, this is not psychotherapy, not in the classical sense. We believe, though, that couples who have to face challenges together grow closer."

Violet snorted. Wilmot glared some more. Ed felt the need to defuse the tension.

"You were about to assign cabins," he said.

"Uh, oh, yeah. So, here are the assignments. Tom and Janet, you guys have cabin number one; George and Lilian, number two; Harry and Gertrude, go in number three, and Rose, you and your sister are in number four." He pointedly avoided looking at Violet. "Ed, you and Ernesto are in number five." He hesitated at that point, staring down at the clipboard he carried. "Uh, Peter and Daryl, you are in cabin number six. You have thirty minutes to get your stuff settled, and we start preparing supper. Any questions?"

Peter Pace raised his hand.

"Yes, Peter," Wilmot said.

"Prepare supper? You mean we have to cook our own meals?"

Wilmot smiled. "I do. That's part of the adventure."

Pace looked around, his face a study in confusion.

"Where do we cook? These cabins look too small to have kitchens."

"Cabin number eight is our community room. It's a combined dining hall and kitchen. We'll all meet there in thirty minutes."

With that, he tucked his clipboard under his arm, turned and walked to the center cabin, leaving them standing by the vans looking confused.

Charles Ray

CHAPTER 5

Ed's relief at learning they would be sleeping in cabins instead of tents was dashed when he learned that the cabins had no electricity or running water, and the toilet was a communal facility, little more than a lean-to over a slit trench, in the trees behind, and thankfully downhill, from the cabins.

Preparing supper had started out in pandemonium. The men stood by looking perplexed as four of the women; Janet Evans stood off to the side looking lost and morose; all tried taking charge and insisting that *their* way of preparing a meal was the best way. It got even more complicated when they realized that they would have to cook on an old wood-burning stove, a device that only Rose and Violet had ever even seen before, putting the two of them in charge by default.

After that, with Violet, as usual, actually running things, things settled down. Ed, Ernesto, and Peter Pace were sent to fetch wood, and the other men were instructed to get out of the way. Rose took charge of explaining how to use the old-fashioned cooking implements, and Violet moved around, overseeing the entire operation.

The meal actually turned out to be quite nice. Rose whipped up a batch of fluffy biscuits, scrambled eggs, and fried slices of ham. She apologized for serving what was normally breakfast fare for supper, but explained that, with the ingredients available, it was the easiest menu to devise. She also apologized for them having to either sit outside and eat or return to their individual cabins to eat alone.

The general consensus was that eating outside, squatting on the ground, would be a good way for the group to begin getting to know each other. Tom Evans, though, insisted on taking his food back to his cabin, and pulled a reluctant Janet along with him. When the couple were out of hearing range, George Lake, a heavyset man in his late fifties, said, "No one's gonna miss that guy. What a downer he is."

"He certainly has that wife of his under control," Lilian, his wife, added.

The Evans were soon forgotten as everyone dug into their food. Conversation was light, consisting mainly of people filling in personal details about themselves, and the meal was soon finished.

Ed, Ernesto, Rose, and Violet stayed behind to clean up the kitchen, while the others trundled off to their cabins to rest up for the next day's activities. They worked in companionly quiet and when the place met with Rose's standards of neatness, they too retired to their cabins, where, despite Ernesto's snoring sounding like a ripsaw, Ed fell into a deep sleep.

He was yanked from sound slumber by the piercing shrill of a whistle from outside the cabin.

Stumbling out of bed, he pulled on his jeans and hiking boots, buttoned his shirt and threw a light jacket over that. Only then did he wake Ernesto, who grumbled that it was still sleep time as far as he was concerned, but who nonetheless got up and dressed.

Ed was rubbing at the raspy stubble on his chin as they stumbled out of the cabin, where they found Wilmot, looking as if he'd just stepped out of a *Men's Health* ad, inappropriately dressed for the chilly morning temperature, in Ed's opinion, in an olive-green tee shirt and camo pants tucked into green canvas and black leather combat boots. Their camping companions, looking as befuddled and disgruntled as Ed felt, were stumbling toward them from their cabins. Only Rose and Violet, early risers back at PVC, looked like the early wake-up call hadn't bothered them. They were both dressed in tan walking slacks, with tan hip-length jackets hugging their hips, and with their heads covered by wide-brim bush hats. Both also carried hiking poles.

"Good morning, campers," Wilmot said in a weak imitation of a drill sergeant. "Welcome to your first day of adventure."

"But, we arrived yesterday," Gertrude Pope said. "Doesn't that count as our first day?"

"You were never in the army, so you wouldn't understand." Wilmot laughed. "The day you arrive at the training site is easy, so it don't count. First day of training, that's when it starts to burn."

Ed could tell the way he recited the words as if he'd memorized them that Wilmot had never served a day in uniform, other than maybe the Boy Scouts. If he had, he'd know that the first day of training, with drill sergeants screaming unfamiliar commands laced with obscenities, and being forced to run everywhere, and drop and do pushups for the most minor infraction of rules of which you were totally ignorant, is the absolute worst day of a person's life. It's designed that way, to make the grueling days that follow bearable. He wouldn't call the man on it, though. That would be rude and unnecessarily hostile. He might mention it to Violet, just in passing. She'd be sure to stick it to him the first time he crossed her.

"So, what's on the agenda for our first day?" Ed asked.

"Glad you asked. First, you'll have breakfast. I'm gonna go easy on you today. I have some breakfast bars and energy drinks to give you. Starting tomorrow, though, you fix your own breakfast, or you don't eat. After we eat, we're going for a nice, easy nature walk, so I can introduce you to the island, and show you some of the training areas."

He passed out two fruit and nut breakfast bars and a pint container of some sickly greenish yellow liquid to each person. The bars were dry and crumbly and tasted to Ed like sugar-coated sawdust, and the flavor of the drink was undecipherable and slightly off. Still, it did fill him, and he had a feeling from the sly look on Wilmot's face when he said they were going on an easy walk, that it would be anything but easy.

After they finished eating, Wilmot inspected everyone to make sure they were appropriately attired, sending Gertrude Pope and, surprisingly, Tom Evans, back to their cabins to change into shoes more appropriate for walking in the wild. Pope had worn low heels and Evans had on a pair of expensive-looking running shoes; good for showing off in a pickup game on the corner, but on rough ground, his feet would've been mincemeat and bruises in a couple of hours.

The two offenders chastened and changed, they set out on a path that ran behind the central cabin.

Just as they entered the woods, Ed heard Janet Evans' voice behind him saying, "I told you those shoes were wrong for this place." Her husband voice dripped with venom. "Shut your trap, or I'll shut it for you," he said in a low, hissing voice. Ed shrugged and sighed. This was shaping up to be an unforgettable day.

The walk reminded Ed of the 40-mile hike he'd had to do in basic training, minus the 70-pound pack and rusty M-1 he'd had to carry. By the time they broke for lunch, and they'd walked the whole time, listening to Wilmot's lecture on how to avoid ticks, not to worry about snakes, but the scorpions that lurked under rotting logs could do almost as much harm, and on, and on, until Ed had tuned him out, concentrating on putting one tired foot in front of the other.

Lunch was a repeat of breakfast, only this time, the energy drink was green, and tasted like it looked, extract of dried stinkweed.

After lunch, more walking until they came to a ledge over a canyon, the floor of which was covered with stunted evergreens and small SUV-sized boulders. A zipline rig had been erected twenty feet back from the edge of the ledge, with the line ending on a small hill on the far side of the canyon.

"Who's up for a little trip down to the bottom of the ledge?" Wilmot asked.

Heads turned, with everyone looking at everyone else. Finally, Gertrude Pope broke the silence. "You mean we have to climb down there?"

"No, I had something a bit more exciting in mind." Wilmot looked at Ed. "Ed, you're looking at the zip rig like you're familiar with it." Ed nodded. "You want to tell your companions what this is?"

"Okay, but I'm a little rusty, so I might not get all the details right."

"No problem, I'll fill anything important that you miss."

"Well, folks, that rig over there is a zip line rig. It's a variation on an old transportation system used in some mountainous areas."

"Oh, oh, I know." Gertrude Pope was jumping and down and raising her hand. "I've seen something like it on the *National Geographic* channel. You slide down the rope in a harness, right?"

"Yeah, that's essentially it."

"Have you ever done it before?"

"When I was in the army, I did jungle survival training in Panama. One of the exercises was to zip line over the *Chagres* River."

"That sounds dangerous." She shivered and hugged herself.

"Sounds more dangerous than it actually is. I remember it as being kind of fun."

Wilmot stepped in front of him. "Then, do you mind going first to demonstrate for the group?"

"What the hell, why not."

Ed followed him to the base of the rig to which the zip line was attached. He took a ride harness and what looked like a bicycle helmet from a green footlocker attached to one of the steel legs and handed them to Ed.

"You need any help with the harness?"

No, I think I can handle it." He could, but it took two tries to get the leg straps straightened out. Once he clicked the helmet's chin strap in place, he turned to Wilmot. "Ready when you are."

Wilmot pulled down the cable and hook and attached it to Ed's shoulder harness. He then placed a hand on his shoulder and walked him to the edge. "When I tap your shoulder, just push away from the cliff," he said.

Ed nodded as Wilmot tapped his shoulder, and as he shoved away from the ledge, yelled over his shoulder, "See you guys on the down side!"

And, away, and down he went. He knew that with the steep angle of the cable, he was descending at nearly 100 miles per hour, or so it felt. He wondered what the landing would be like, and then took a deep breath. The tour company would naturally have some soft landing. Pancaking customers into the ground after a 500-foot ride would be bad for business. He glanced around and down. The ground seemed to be coming up at him faster than it should, but the far wall of the canyon was moving at a much slower rate. He tried to tell himself that was subjective because of the differences in distances or something along those lines, and that he should be enjoying the ride, and then he came to a jerking, swinging halt, suspended two feet above a platform of what looked to him like

Styrofoam mattresses staked to the ground. A sign on the frame to which the cable was attached instructed him to unhook the hook from his harness and push the red button on the panel next to the sign. When he did so, the hook began a sedate crawl back up the cable. That's when he noticed the thin, rubber-covered line attached to the hook. A pulley system that retrieved the hook for the next rider.

He removed his helmet and took a deep breath. It had been a short ride, but one hell of a rush. He smiled. No way was he telling Violet, or Wilmot, that he'd enjoyed it.

He watched the others, one by one, come zipping down the cable, although none of them seemed to be moving as fast as he felt he was moving. Another subjective impression, he thought.

When the last person, Janet Evans, unhooked her harness and removed her helmet, Wilmot called down for them to wait near the base of the zip line for him. He then turned around and jumped off the ledge. There was a collective gasp from everyone and then cheers and applause when he arced out and back with his feet planted firmly against the rock wall, holding a rope in his hand that suddenly dropped from his waist until it reached a point a few feet from the canyon floor.

"Well, I'll be danged," Ed said. "He's rappelling down. I must admit, this fella knows how to put on a show."

"I wonder if he'll show us how to do that," Gertrude said. "That looks like it's almost as much fun as this zip line thingy."

"It's not a *thingy*, Gertrude," her husband said. "How many times do I have to tell you to be precise when you speak?"

"Oh, hush up, Harry, they know what I'm talking about."

Harry Pope mumbled something unintelligible and turned back the quiet conversation he was having with Tom Evans.

While Ed wasn't as put off at the way she spoke as her husband was, he, too, wished she'd keep her mouth shut. He didn't mind—in fact, he liked—the zip line, but rappelling down the side of a rock wall from a height that if you fell before you were less than ten feet from the bottom could be fatal, and even from ten feet or less, if the ground you landed upon was rocky, could be harmful, and was always uncomfortable, especially when you were doing it backwards, and had to crane your head around to see where you were going. Of course, that way was preferable to the way the Australians did it; face forward, your body at a ninety-degree angle to the wall. Leave it to the Aussies to come up with the most dangerous way to do something.

Unfortunately, Wilmot's hearing was sharp. He had heard her. When he reached the bottom, he took of his rappelling gear and walked over to the group.

"As a matter of fact, Gertrude," he said. "You guys did such a good job on the zip line *thingy*." And, at that point, he shot a glare at her husband. "I think I will give you a few lessons in rappelling . . . not on this wall, it's too high . . . but, we have a beginner's course set up on a ledge not far from here."

"Oh, goody." Gertrude clapped her hands and jumped up and down.

Her husband glared at her.

Ed sighed.

"We're not going to do the Australian rappel, are we?" he asked.

Wilmot looked surprised. "You rappelled in the army, too?"

"Yeah, a few times. I did not like the Australian rappel."

"That one is a challenge, what with having to do something that the mind rebels at. But, you know, it's the easiest and safest way to descend a rock face. Less chance of getting your feet tangled or stuck. But, it's too hard for beginners, so we stick to the traditional way." He cocked his head and regarded Ed for a few seconds. "I get the feeling that you don't like either way."

"You are a very perceptive young man. The thing is, I'm not too fond of heights."

"But, you did the zip line so well."

"There are exceptions to everything. Maybe it's because on the sip line, you're moving so fast, you don't have time to think about how high up you are. And, you can always just look up and wait for the ride to be over, unlike rappelling, where you have to look all around you the whole way down to keep from screwing up."

Wilmot nodded his head. "I guess that makes sense. You will try it, though, won't you?"

Ed made a quiet growling sound in his throat. "Yeah, I suppose so."

"Yeah, Ed, you don't want to be a wet blanket, do you?" Violet asked.

"It's not that. I just want to show you newbies that it can be done, so you don't pee your pants when you try it. If an old geezer like me can do it, it should be a snap for the rest of you."

Ernesto, who had been quiet for most of the morning, speaking only when spoken to, mostly by Rose, who was never more than an arm's length from him, laughed. "Hell, don't let him fool you. Old Ed here is pretty tough. He once went up against a woman who was tryin' to shoot him. Got her, too, he did."

"Did not," Ed said. "I just ducked until the police arrived and arrested her. Luckily, she was a lousy shot."

Harry Pope looked at Ed, his eyes narrowed to slits. "What the hell were you doing to be shot at by anyone?"

"He was investigating a murder. Turned out, she'd killed her husband."

"I thought you said you were retired from the defense department?"

"Oh, he is," Rose said. "But, he investigates the occasional crime as sort of a hobby."

Ed shrugged. "Mostly, I sort of stumble into a situation. It's not like I'm some kind of private investigator or anything. When you're retired, you have a lot of time on your hands, and Ernesto and I can only play so many rounds of golf a week."

Everyone but Pope laughed. He looked skeptical. "So, you're one of those nosy parkers who's always sticking his nose in other people's business?"

Ed was beginning to develop a strong dislike for the man but decided not to push it. "Only if their business bumps into me," he said. "Thankfully, we'll all be so busy this week trying not to break an ankle, or look like a fool, I don't think that's gonna happen."

"Good," Wilmot said. "Now that we have that settled, let's go over to the rappelling station."

CHAPTER 6

The rappelling, down a near-vertical, fifty-foot rock wall, using the traditional technique, turned out not to be too bad. Ed was reluctant to admit that he'd actually enjoyed it, especially as Wilmot used him to demonstrate correct techniques, and complimented him on how much he'd remembered after over forty years. Even Violet, never one to be free with compliments, patted him on the back after his third trip down the wall.

They stopped for lunch, more nut bars and energy drinks—the taste was beginning to become bearable—seated on the ground in a moss-covered clearing in the pine and oak trees fifty yards from the rappelling station.

Ed, Ernesto, Violet, and Rose sat in a group off to the side of the others, munching idly at the bars, and washing them down with the drink. The rappelling had drained them so much that no one, other than the irrepressible Rose, felt like talking. Rose, though, never seemed to run out of topics of conversation. Ed's performance on the rappel was her subject *du jour*.

"Ed," she mumbled around a mouthful of energy bar. "You were amazing. You came down that cliff like you've been doing that kind of thing regularly, and not just something you did a few times decades ago."

Ed washed down the gritty bar and nodded at her. "It's kind of like riding a bike. You never really forget."

Ernesto looked around at the others in their group. Everyone looked tired, but most were smiling. The exceptions were Tom and Janet Evans. She looked sad, and he looked angry.

"Looks like not everyone is enjoying it," he said.

Ed looked in the direction Ernesto was looking.

"Yeah, that is one unhappy couple. I wonder what's up with them?"

"Maybe I should talk to them," Rose said.

"Maybe we both should," Ed said.

"Maybe you two should just leave them alone," Violet said.

Ed stood and frowned down at her. "Look, we've got to spend the rest of the week with these people. It's a good idea to get to know them, and . . . well, it's just a good idea to know the people you're working with. Come on, Rose, let's go talk to them."

Rose took his arm, shooting a harsh look at her older sister.

"Ernesto," Violet said. "You really need to have a talk with that sister of mine."

"Hey, don't get me in the middle of this sibling rivalry you have going," he said. "Besides, I kinda agree with Ed. If that couple has a problem it could affect all of us. We're in pretty close quarters around here, or haven't you noticed."

She made a raspberry sound and went back to eating her lunch.

As Ed and Rose approached the couple, the woman smiled wanly, but the man regarded them with icy blue eyes.

"Hi, Tom and Janet, right," Ed said. "I'm Ed, and this is Rose. Where are you folks from?"

"We live in Fairfax City," the woman said. The man glared at her. "Yes, I'm Janet, and this is my husband, Tom. Are you guys from Virginia, too?"

"Janet, don't be so nosy," Tom Evans said. "It's not polite."

She shrank away from him as if he'd hit her. Ed didn't fail to notice that he had his fists clenched when he spoke. He figured that at some point, he *had* hit her, which made his cheeks hot. Men who hit their wives were, in his universe, almost as bad as child molesters, deserving of a trip to the woodshed.

"In this environment," he said. "It's not only polite, it's pretty much necessary."

"Why is that?" Evans asked in a hostile tone. "Did we sign away our right to privacy when we came on this trip?"

"I think I understand what he means, dear. This is a challenging week, and we'll have to work together, so we need to know each other."

"I didn't ask you," Evans snapped. He turned back to Ed. "Look, I'm not a very talkative person, and I don't like sharing personal information with strangers. You understand?"

It was, in effect, a dismissal. Rose opened her mouth to say something, but Ed nudged her gently in the side.

"Sure, no offense. Just thought it'd be a good idea if we knew each other better; but suit yourself. Come on, Rose."

He took her by the arm and led her away.

When they were out of earshot, she leaned in to him and said, "He's a real dick, that one."

Ed looked wide-eyed at her. He agreed with her assessment but had never heard her use such vulgarity. She was right on the mark, though, he thought; Tom Evans was a real dick.

Charles Ray

CHAPTER 7

The afternoon was spent back near the cabins, running a military-style obstacle course, in which Ed was again used as a demonstrator by virtue of being the only member of the group with prior military experience.

By the end of the afternoon, he was soaking wet with sweat, but felt invigorated. It hadn't hurt that all the women were fussing over him and lauding his prowess, a word that hadn't been used to describe him for many a year.

After washing the dust off his body in the men's shower, a canvas and steel frame facility with a sign that said, 'Men's Latrine,' located behind the cabins on the north side—the women's latrine was behind the cabins at the south end—he and Ernesto went to join Rose, Violet, and Gertrude in the kitchen to help prepare supper.

The first thing Ed noticed when he entered was that Violet looked a bit more morose than usual, which he found *unusual* because he was sure he'd seen her smiling several times during the afternoon's activities, and at one point, when Ernesto got his feet tangled in the auto tires while trying to beat Ed to the end, she had actually laughed.

Ed waited until Rose and Ernesto were busy at the stove, deep in conversation, and he walked over to the table where Violet sat, looking glum and peeling potatoes.

"How I remember having to do that when I was in basic training," he said.

"Doing what?" She spoke without looking up at him.

"Peeling potatoes. A grueling job before the mechanical potato peeler was invented. We recruits used to be assigned KP, that's kitchen police, duty, and peeling the potatoes that were served at every meal was one of the tasks we had to perform. The only thing I hated worse than peeling potatoes was having to clean out the grease trap."

She put the potato she'd been peeling down, jabbed the peeler into it, and turned to face him. "You know, Ed, you lived a pretty full and interesting life before coming to PVC."

He sat down beside her.

"Yeah, I suppose that's true, but what does that have to do with why you've been so mopey lately."

"Oh, it's that danged bet we made with Jason," she said.

"Why are you worried about that? Hey, if we lose and have to do his stupid ad, at least we'll be famous."

"I know, but it means we will have lost."

"Hey, you win some and you lose some."

"That's easy enough for you to say. You've done enough interesting things, that you can take losing in stride. Do you know t hat before coming to PVC, Rose and I had never done anything worthwhile? We never got married and had families, never really had any kind of meaningful jobs . . . even when we did the obligatory young lady's trip to Europe, we were chaperoned."

"Sure, but look at you now," Ed said. "Rappelling, zip lining, and all kinds of things."

"I know, I know, but the thought of losing . . . well, it makes me kind of crazy."

"You mean losing that silly bet?"

"Yes, I mean that silly bet. Do you know I've never won anything in my whole life?"

"Have you bet much?"

"No, this is the first time."

Ed tried to stifle it, but he couldn't help himself. He laughed.

"You *are* kidding, right? Haven't you ever tried those scratch off cards that come in the magazines sometimes?"

She shook her head. Her eyes glistened with unshed tears. It was the most vulnerable he'd ever seen her, and he found it disturbing. "It's not funny, Ed. I cannot help it if I led a sheltered life. That's one of the reasons I wanted to come on this trip. To be able to let my hair down. I don't want to lose this bet, and it has nothing to do with the stupid ad."

He patted her shoulder.

"If it makes you feel any better, I sort of feel the same way. I *hate* losing."

She smiled weakly.

"You're just saying that to make me feel better."

"No, really. Have you seen me smile where Jason could see it?"

"Now that you mention it, no. So, I'm not being crazy>"

"Not at all. It's a normal human emotion. Look, let's make a pact. I'll watch you, and you watch me. If we seen either looking like he or she's having fun, we'll say something like, oh, horse feathers."

The smile got broader.

"Sounds like a plan to me."

Ed held out his hand. She took it and held it for a long time.

"Game on, partner?" He winked at her.

"Game on." She winked back.

Charles Ray

CHAPTER 8

After supper, while the Tom and Janet Evans, at his insistence, retired straight away to their cabin, the rest of the group sat around a fire Wilmot built in front of the cooking cabin, and resumed getting to know each other. The mood was light, with Harry Pope chiding his wife for her inappropriate attire—she again wore heels—and her blushing and laughing about it.

"I'm assuming that with tomorrow being Sunday," she said. "We will have at least part of the day to just sit back and reflect." She looked hopefully at Wilmot.

"Come on, Gertrude," Pope said. "This is no time to be thinking about dressing up for Sunday idleness."

A fleeting look of hurt flashed across her face, quickly replaced with her trademark smile. Ed felt like going over to Pope and kicking him in the balls.

Wilmot shot Pope a dirty look. "As a matter of fact," he said. "Tomorrow morning is for rest and reflection. So, feel free to dress up if it makes you feel better. In the afternoon, though, we resume our rigorous schedule."

Gertrude's smile grew wider, while her husband's expression turned stormy.

"I'm not paying a hundred bucks a day per person to be mollycoddling people," he said. "I came here to test myself, to find my limits."

"Testing your limits involves more than physical activity, Harry." Wilmot dropped the drill sergeant voice, replacing it with the long-suffering guidance counselor. "Sometimes we have to tap into our mental and spiritual sides to really get to know who we are."

"Hmph, sounds like psycho-babble bullshit to me." Pope folded his arms across his chest and glared at Wilmot.

"You've only been here one full day, Harry. Give it time." Wilmot clapped his hands. "Now, who knows a good campfire story?"

CHAPTER 9

Sunday morning, Ed rolled out of bed feeling conflicted. On the one hand, he *was* enjoying the trip—sort of—but, on the other, he would've liked to be able to choose better companions. Ernesto, Rose, and Violet were okay, as were Peter Pace, Daryl Drum, George and Lilian Lake, Janet Evans, and Gertrude Pope. He was even beginning to warm up to Jason Wilmot. As for Tom Evans and Harry Pope, though, the less time he spent around them, the better. They were sour, abusive to their wives, and generally obstructive, making him wonder why they even wanted to come on a trip like this.

Oh well, he thought, I'll just have to find ways to avoid them.

After pulling on his pants and shoes he went out to the men's latrine and washed his face and upper body and brushed his teeth. It was a rudimentary bit of toiletry, which he called a monkey bath, but it did at least make him feel better. He then went back inside, roused Ernesto, and finished dressing.

When Ernesto had finished his own toilet, they went to the kitchen cabin, where they found Rose and Violet busy over the stove while Lilian Lake peeled potatoes. She hummed as she worked.

"Wow," Ed said. "A recruit who likes the second worst job on KP."

Lillian looked up at him, a puzzled frown on her round face. "What's a recruit, what's KP, and what job are you referring to?"

Ed explained the concept of kitchen police, the army structure, and the two worst jobs that a recruit could be assigned to, besides cleaning out a field latrine, and then finished by saying, "I've never seen anyone humming while peeling potatoes,"

"Oh, I find kitchen work, even things like peeling vegetables, quite relaxing," Lilian said. "Sometimes, George and I do it together, and we sing old campfire songs while we work."

"Now, that," Ed said. "Is what I call a happy home life."

"Oh, George and I love doing things together. Right now, he's out in the woods finding flowers to liven up our Sunday breakfast."

As if he'd been on the same brain wave-length as his wife, George Lake walked into the cabin carrying an armload of yellow, blue, and red flowers. Like his wife, he had a broad smile on his face. "Top of the morning to all," he said. He crossed the room and kissed his wife's cheeks. Then, he held the flowers out for her to inspect. "What do you think, dear? Will these brighten up our humble repast?"

"Those will do just fine, hon. But, you'd better find a container and put them in some water so they don't wilt."

Watching he two of them interacting with other, Ed thought to the way he and his late wife had been together—not quite as mushy, but close. At times like this, he really missed her.

But, you can't relive the past, he thought. He shook himself and turned his attention back to his current companions.

"What do you make of the Popes and the Evans?" he asked Lilian.

She stopped peeling again, and pinched the bridge of her nose, crossing her eyes to look at her fingers.

"Well, I don't like speaking ill of other people," she said. "Gertrude and Janet are really nice people, but they drew short straws in the spouse department."

"Yeah, neither of those gentlemen would make it on my Christmas list."

She leaned forward and lowered her voice. "You know, I think Tom Evans . . . hits Janet," she whispered.

"Really? Why do you say that?" Ed kept his own voice low as well.

"I volunteer at a women's shelter in Germantown. I've seen literally hundreds of abused women, so I recognize the signs. Did you notice how she cringes when he speaks to her, and that she always wears long sleeves? Those are two classic signs of a woman who is being abused."

Ed had suspected that Evans was abusive, probably even physically so, but it had been more on *his* behavior than on his victim's. He decided that he'd keep a closer eye on Mr. Evans.

"So, what's to be done about it?" he asked.

Lilian shook her head. "Unless the victim decides to admit that she's being abused and commits to doing something about it, I'm afraid there's really not much anyone can do. Do you know that every minute in this country, 20 people are physically abused by their partner?" she picked the potato up and began peeling it with a vengeance. "One in seven men are abused, but it's terrible when you look at the statistics for women. One in four women have been victims of severe physical violence from an intimate partner. Violence by an intimate partner accounts for fifteen percent of all violent crime."

"Holy crap," Ed said. "I didn't realize it was so bad."

"Men, women and children, but especially women and children, because they are more vulnerable, are being abused at alarming rates. And do you know that only a third of those who are abused ever get medical care?"

"What! How the heck can that be?"

"Sometimes the abused partner is too ashamed to report the incident, as if somehow they're to blame. Of course, with children, it's the same thing. The non-abusing partner often makes excuses or covers up for the abuser."

"Dang. I guess I'll have to keep my eyes open around Mr. Evans. What about Harry Pope? You mentioned him as not being all there. Is he abusing his wife as well?"

"Verbally, not physically," she said. "Harry's the classic bully. In fact, most abusers are bullies, and like bullies everywhere, they pick on the weak, and only do what they think they can get away with. In Harry's case, he seems to get off on publicly humiliating Gertrude, but I think he's too big a coward to ever lay a hand on her. She takes the verbal stuff, but I don't think she's submit to physical abuse."

Ed shook his head. "I'm beginning to think that this will be an interesting, and not necessarily in a nice way, week."

Lilian looked up. Her eyes widened. In a voice so low, Ed almost didn't hear, she said, "Speak of the devil, Harry just came in."

Pope walked past the table where Ed and Lilian sat without acknowledging them, directly to Rose and Violet at the stove.

"When will breakfast be ready? I'm starved," he said.

Violet turned and waved a grease-streaked spatula at him, causing him to jump backwards to keep from getting hot grease spatter on his face. "It will be ready when it's ready," she said. "Now, unless you're here to help prepare it, get your carcass out of my face."

Pope seemed to shrink a full size.

"S-sorry," he said. "It's just that I'm hungry. If I was at home I would've eaten my breakfast by now."

"Just in case you haven't noticed, you're not *at* home. Now help us or hump it."

Meekly, he turned and then seemed to notice Ed and Lilian for the first time.

"Mind if I join you guys?"

"Have a seat," Lilian said. "You can help me peel the potatoes."

He held his hands up, palms out. "I don't think you want me to do that. I'm all thumbs in the kitchen. That's Gertrude's domain."

"Speaking of Gertrude," she said. "Where is she? She said last night that she'd come help me."

"She was still burrowed under the covers, sleeping when I left. I guess she decided to sleep in this morning."

Lilian stopped peeling and looked at him, her brow knitted. "That doesn't sound like her. She was really excited about helping prepare Sunday breakfast."

"You just met her. How can you say what does or does not sound like her?"

The look she gave him was icy. "I'm a pretty good judge of character. I think I probably know your wife better than you do."

"Hah! What are you some kind of shrink or profiler?"

"Something like that." Her tone was getting colder and colder. She stood. "I'm going to your cabin and talk to her."

Pope's expression was noncommittal. "Suit yourself." He looked at Ed. "Hey, Ed, right, is there any coffee?"

His tone was preemptory and demanding. Ed wanted to slap him, but he let his better nature rule. "Yeah, on the table there in the corner."

Pope went over, filled a cup, and came back to the table. He sat across from Ed, his elbows resting on the table, and blew on his coffee. The last thing Ed wanted to do at that moment was to engage him in conversation, so he picked up Lilian's discarded potato peeler, took a spud from the bowl, and began peeling. He held the potato by one end and began peeling from the tip at the other, sliding the blade of the peeler carefully underneath the outer skin and pulling it gently around, turning the potato at the same time, in an effort to take the entire peel off in one piece. He hummed a mindless tune as he concentrated intensely on keeping the peeler steady, and very quickly blocked Pope's presence from his mind.

He had just about reached the bottom of the potato, rewarded with a tangled coil of brown peel resting on the back of his right hand as he tried to work the peeler around for the last slice, when the door to the cabin slammed open, causing him to jerk and cut the peel off with a dime-sized piece still attached to the potato.

"Dang it," he said. "Almost made it."

He looked toward the door, where Lilian stood, her right hand on her chest, and a frightened look in her eyes. She was breathing hard, as if she'd been running.

"She's gone," she said when she'd finally caught her breath.

"Who's gone?" Ed asked.

"Gertrude. She's not in her cabin."

Pope put his cup down and turned to face her.

"She's probably just at that, what did Jason call it, latrine, yeah, latrine. She's probably at the latrine getting cleaned up."

Lilian advanced on him, her eyes blazing. "She. Is. Not. At. The. Latrine," she said. "I checked. She's not there, and she's not in the cabin. She's gone."

"Maybe she went for a walk in the forest."

"I don't think so. Her walking shoes were under the bed."

Pope smiled, not a mirthful smile at all, Ed thought. "So, you like snooping around, do you? What else did you find?"

Something in the way he asked the question put Ed's senses on alert. He couldn't quite figure out what about it bothered him, only that it did.

"Something strange," Lilian said. "At first, it did look like she was still under the covers, but when she didn't answer me, I pulled them back. Do you want to know what I found?"

"I suspect you'll tell me whether I want to know or not."

"A bunch of rolled-up clothing, making it look like someone was under those covers, that's what I found."

Pope's left eyebrow twitched upward. He frowned. But, just as his smile conveyed no happiness, his frown was a put-on. Ed saw no surprise or any other emotion in his eyes.

"Rolled up clothing? What in the hell . . . looks like she finally did what she's been threatening to do for years; she's up and left me."

Ed put the potato and peeler down and leaned forward. "That makes no sense," he said.

"Why not. She's not there, and she had her bed made up to make me think she was still in it. What other explanation could there be?"

What other explanation indeed? Ed's mind was abuzz with possibilities, all of which involved underhanded behavior on the part of Harry Pope.

"Where would she go? The ferry's not due back until the end of our stay, and it's too far to the mainland to swim."

Pope shrugged. "Hell, I don't know. Maybe she found some local with a boat, or maybe she's hiding out in the woods, waiting for me to leave."

And, maybe, Ed thought, you've done something to her, or, given Lilian Lake's assessment of him, had something done to her.

One way or another, he intended to find out.

CHAPTER 10

"I don't know, Ed," Jason Wilmot said. "Before we call the authorities, shouldn't we try and find her ourselves?"

Sunday breakfast was somber at first. Lilian told everyone as they arrived at the kitchen of Gertrude's absence. Then, the mood turned to excitement when Ed suggested that they call the police and report her missing.

"We don't know this area," Ed said. "We could get more people lost out looking for her."

"The island's not that big, although there are a couple of pretty wild areas. Besides, we have the drivers, both of whom are from around here. They could each guide a group."

Ed knew that Wilmot was just worried about the effect involving the authorities might have on his business, but he had to concede that he did make a good point. If Gertrude was just crouching somewhere in the brush to upset her husband, they would be diverting the authorities from possibly real emergencies.

"Okay," he said. "We'll search, but if we've found nothing by noon, we call in the cops."

Wilmot didn't look happy with that, but finally nodded his agreement. "I'll take one group," he said. "And, since you have military experience, you lead the other. I'll ask the drivers to go along since they know the area. When do you want to get started?"

Ed looked at his watch. It was already half past nine. "By the time we can get organized, it'll be lunch time. Why don't we start organizing the groups, and giving them instructions, and then after lunch, we start the search."

He deliberately phrased it as a statement rather than a question to forestall any objections Wilmot might have, but the guide simply nodded and began assigning people to either his group or Ed's.

He put Ernesto, Tom Evans and George Lake in his group, and assigned Peter Pace, Daryl Wilson, and Harry Pope to Ed's. The drivers, looking confused at all the fuss were called in. Joseph Nystrom, a fiftyish man with a cantaloupe paunch and two front teeth missing, was assigned to Ed, while Wilmot took Larry Murdock, who looked to be in his mid-forties, and in even worse shape than Nystrom, for his group.

"Okay, folks," Wilmot said. "Right after lunch, we'll start searching for Mrs. Pope. My group will take the north side of the island, and Ed's the south. Be advised that there are a few bogs on the island that can swallow you if you're not careful, so watch where you walk, and, for God's sake, people, stay together, and follow your group leader's instructions. Now, are there any questions?"

No one had any, which surprised Ed. Usually, in situations like this, there would be dozens of questions, but everyone seemed in a state of shock, everyone, that is, except Harry Pope and Tom Evans, both of whom seemed to take the whole thing in stride.

Because Ed suspected that Pope had done something to his wife, he was not surprised at his reaction, or lack of reaction, but he was confused at

Evans' lack of concern. Could the man be that uncaring of others, he thought to himself, that a woman missing in the relative wilds of the island not trigger the slightest sign of sympathy?

He shrugged mentally. Apparently, Tom Evans cared for no one.

Charles Ray

CHAPTER 11

They searched until the sun was low in the sky and the long shadows in the trees limited visibility. Reluctantly, Ed led his group back to the cabins, arriving a few minutes after Wilmot's group, who were standing in front of the kitchen.

"Did you guys see anything?" Wilmot asked.

"Nothing," Ed replied. "We saw footprints in the areas where we were training, but there's no way to tell if any of them were made at another time. I think we're gonna need to call in professionals."

"I tell you, I think she found someone with a boat and went back to the mainland," Pope said.

Both Ed and Wilmot frowned at him.

"Are you willing to take that chance with your wife's life?" Wilmot asked. "I'm afraid I agree with Ed on this, now. I'm calling Bar Harbor and reporting Gertrude as a missing person."

"While you're doing that," Tom Evans said. "I could do for a cup of coffee. Who's with me?"

Ed's throat did feel a bit dry, despite having taken a bottle of water with him, so he agreed.

"Okay, we'll have coffee while you go make that call, Jason," he said.

Wilmot nodded and trotted off toward his cabin. Ed turned and followed the others into the kitchen, where the women were busy preparing supper. Everyone, save Evans, went to the sideboard and poured himself a cup of coffee. He sat at the table and snapped at his wife to bring him a cup.

She was standing at the sink, washing lettuce leaves, but at the sound of her husband's sharply-worded command, dropped the head of lettuce she'd been holding and began wiping her wet hands on her skirt. Violet put a hand on her arm.

"You keep working on that lettuce, Janet," she said. She then turned and glared across the room at Evans. "You don't look like your legs or arms are broken. You want coffee, you get it yourself like everyone else is doing."

His face turning red, Evans stood and braced himself on the table. "Who the hell are you to be interfering in my family life, you old bag, I ought to—"

Ed reached him the same time that Ernesto did. They flanked him. Ed put a hand, not too gently, on his shoulder.

"Cool down, friend," he said. His voice was as cold as ice. "That's our friend you're talking to, and frankly, I don't like you calling her names."

Evans looked from Ed to Ernesto. His body tensed, and his lips quivered.

"No offense, guys," he said. "But, she's got no business interfering in my family life."

"I don't know about that," Ernesto said. "From the looks of things, your wife's busy helpin' get supper ready, and you not wantin' to haul your lazy carcass over to get your own coffee is inconviencin' the rest of us."

"Hey, no need for getting nasty." Evans' voice had a plaintive, whiny tone.

"The shoe pinches when it's on the other foot, doesn't it?" Ed asked. "Now, why don't you get your coffee like everyone else is doing?"

He tried staring Ed down. Ed, though, kept his expression neutral, a difficult task when all he wanted to do was punch the obnoxious man in the face. Finally, Evans shrugged, stood and walked to the sideboard. He frowned as he poured coffee into a cup, frowned harder when his wife kept her back to him, and then returned to the table where he sat the cup down so hard, some of the coffee splashed onto the table.

"You'd better clean that up," Violet said. "We don't want to attract pests with spills."

He turned and glared at her.

"I'd do what she says if I was you," Ed said. "You might think Ernesto and I were protecting her just now, but you'd be wrong. You get on Violet's bad side, and it could be hazardous to your health."

Evans' brows rose as he looked at Ed. Ed could see that he wanted an explanation but decided to let him think about it.

Wilmot walked in, went to the sideboard, got his own coffee, and then joined them at the table.

"I called the state police station at Bar Harbor," he said. He blew on his coffee and took a sip. "They can't get a man out here to look into it before tomorrow."

"Are there any local police?" Ed asked.

"Here on the island? No. And, since the island's not part of any municipality, it would be either the county or state police who have jurisdiction. I figured it best to call the state police because they have more resources."

"Good idea." Ed looked over at Harry Pope, who was standing near the stove drinking his coffee and watching the women prepare the meal. "Say, Harry, do you mind if I take a look at your cabin?"

Pope looked suspiciously at him. "Why do you want to do that?"

"It might give me some idea where Gertrude might've gotten off to. I imagine the state police will want to do the same thing, so I thought it might be easier if someone you knew did it first."

After several seconds, during which he stared curiously at Ed, Pope finally nodded. "I suppose you're right. If you find something useful, we can turn it over to the cops when they arrive. Sure, go ahead and look."

"You should come with me," Ed said. "I wouldn't be comfortable going through your things without you there."

"I should go, too," Lilian said. "I might notice something about a woman's possessions that a man would miss."

"Sure, come along. Any objections, Harry?"

Pope put his cup down and shook his head. "Nah, knock yourselves out. Come on, then, let's get this over with."

CHAPTER 12

The walk to the Pope's cabin, number three, didn't take long, and the man didn't seem interested in making conversation during the walk. When they reached the cabin, he pushed the door open and stepped aside to allow Ed and Lilian to enter, then walked in behind them.

The inside of Pope's cabin was the same as the one Ed and Ernesto stayed in, except the beds seemed a bit farther apart, and only one was made up. Ed assumed that the rumpled bed with the pile of clothes on it and the coverlet folded back was the one Gertrude Pope had slept in. It was farthest from the door, against the far wall on the right. Their suitcases were stacked neatly against the wall on the left.

Ed inspected the bed first, finding nothing of interest. The bottom sheet was unwrinkled and the pillow still fully fluffed. A dog-eared romance novel lay aslant on the night table between the two beds. Lilian, while Ed looked the bed over, went to the stacked cases.

"Which one is Gertrude's?" she asked Pope.

"The one on the bottom," he said.

She slid the top suitcase aside and, kneeling, opened the bottom one. Ed had finished inspecting the bed, so he stood behind her and watched as she first looked at the neatly folded and stacked items in the suitcase, and then began lifting them out, one by one. When she'd completely emptied the suitcase, she just as carefully put everything back.

She stood and rubbed her back and knees.

"I think I'm getting a bit too old for this," she said. "Kneeling like that hurt my old knees."

"I know what you mean," Ed said. "I have problems bending over to tie my shoes in the morning."

"You should buy slip-ons," Pope said gruffly. "A lot easier on the back."

Ed didn't want to engage the man in casual conversation but decided to be gracious. "Not a bad idea, thanks." To Lilian, he said, "Anything of interest in the suitcase?"

"Everything," she said.

"You mind explaining that."

"Well, her . . . unmentionables and makeup are all there, as are her pajamas. It looks to me like, *if* she left, she left in what she was wearing last night."

"Hm," Ed said. "That is interesting." He wanted to tell her why, but not with Pope listening. He turned to the man who watched them with a half-smile on his face. "Well, thanks for letting us have a look. Nothing of interest here, I guess. You going back to the kitchen?"

Pope shook his head. "Nah, I think I'll hang out here for a while. Call me when supper's ready."

Ed thought him arrogant but was just as glad he wasn't going back with them. It would give him to further question Lilian. "Okay, will do."

He took a confused looking Lilian by the elbow and guided her out of the cabin.

"What was that all about?" she asked when they were outside and a few steps from the door.

"I wanted to ask you what you meant about her things, but I didn't want Harry to hear," he said.

"Ah, I see. You think there's been foul play, and he's the perp, right?"

"Uh, well, I don't actually think of it in those old B-movie terms, but, yes, I have a feeling Gertrude Pope did not leave here of her own free will."

"Because of her leaving all her things behind, right?"

"Yeah. I just can't imagine a woman walking out on her husband and leaving all her clothes behind like that."

Lilian smiled. "There is that," she said. "But, in the short time I knew Gertrude, the thing I can't imagine is her leaving without her makeup. She's a lovely person, but a really vain one, and all her makeup is in her suitcase. No way she'd leave without it."

Ed rubbed at his chin.

"So, we're agreed, she didn't leave of her free will, but that leaves the question of where she is and what happened to her. I think maybe her husband did something to her."

"I don't think so." Lilian shook her head. "At least not directly. Like I said before, I know his type. He's a coward, and he's the kind who would never get his own hands dirty."

"You're saying he hired someone to . . . what, kill his wife?"

"He wouldn't be the first husband to do so," she said. "And, what better place to do it. Out here on this island, we're in effect cut off from civilization. Imagine it; a boat comes under cover of darkness, the killer, or killers, slip ashore, grab Gertrude, kill her, take her body out to sea and dump it, and then go back to the mainland."

"Wow, Lilian. You should be a mystery writer. That is a fantastic scenario you've come up with."

'What? You don't think it could've happened that way?"

"No, as a matter of fact, I think that's exactly the way it could've happened."

CHAPTER 13

After supper, Pope went back to his cabin, leaving the rest of the group to spend the evening speculating on what might have happened to his wife, ranging from his strangling her and burying her in one of the bogs on the island to him hiring a gang of mobsters who kidnapped her and dumped her body in the Atlantic. What no one could come up with was why the man would want to get rid of his wife. While George Lake, basing his assumption on what his wife, Lilian, had told him about Harry Pope and the way he treated his wife, was the lone holdout, insisting that she'd just decided on a whim to leave the rat, and was probably enjoying herself in a tavern in Bar Harbor as they spoke.

The only one of the group who refused to join in the conversation, who, in fact, sat in a corner scowling at them until they broke up and went back to their respective cabins, was Tom Evans. He had, at one point, even ordered his wife to stop gossiping about a person she hardly knew, was surprised when she stuck her tongue out at him and continued to engage Rose in conversation and spent the rest of the evening in the corner silently fuming.

Jason Wilmot finally got them to turn in around midnight, after announcing that the planned activities for Monday morning would be put on hold until they knew how extensive and intensive any police investigation would be. He'd been informed by cell phone during dinner that a policeman would be arriving by boat shortly after 9:00 am, so there was no sense in planning any morning activity. They would, though, do something in the afternoon, he insisted, even if it was nothing but another nature hike, for he was adamant that they get their money's worth from the trip.

The next morning, the boat, an 18-foot Boston whaler, piloted by man who looked to be in his eighties, if not older, arrived with two passengers.

One was a tall, broad-shouldered police officer, wearing a Smoky Bear hat, dark green jacket over greenish-gray trousers and shiny shoes, with a Heckler & Koch HK45 LEM .45 caliber automatic in a shiny black leather holster. On his left shoulder was the insignia of the state police, a circle inside of which was a farmer and a sailor flanking an elk lying down beneath an evergreen tree. A ribbon at the top had the words State Police, and a banner beneath the moose read Maine. Above the tree was the North Star, beneath which was the word 'Dirigo.' He wore his badge over his left breast, and over the right was a brass tag with his name, Bosley. The other was a beautiful German shepherd, wearing a black leather harness with the words 'K-9 Unit' in white letters on both sides. The dog stayed at the man's left, not touching, but not too far away. It was on a leash, but the man held it loosely in his left hand. His right hand held the handle of a small roll-on suitcase.

Ed, Ernesto, and Lilian had accompanied Wilmot to the dock to meet him.

They had just arrived at the end of the pier as the pilot was securing the boat to one of the pilings and steadying it to allow his two passengers to get off. Once on the pier, the policeman let go of the suitcase, and touched a finger to the brim of his hat. The old man, retrieved his lines and skillfully maneuvered the boat around and headed back toward Bar Harbor.

The man and his dog walked briskly to where they waited.

"I'm Trooper Nelson Bosley from the state police barracks in Ellsworth," he said. "Which one of you is Jason Wilmot?"

"That would be me," Wilmot said.

Bosley looked from Wilmot to each of the others, pausing for a second or two one each as if committing their faces to memory. He let go of the suitcase again and touched a finger to his hat when he looked at Lilian.

"I hope your vehicle has room for Hercules and me," he said.

"An Econoline van. With just the four of us and the driver, you and your dog will have all the room you need."

Bosley didn't move. He stood, looking from Wilmot to the others. After ten seconds, Ed realized that Wilmot hadn't picked up on the trooper's subtle signal that he wanted to know who the extra people were.

"I'm Ed Lazenby," Ed said, stepping forward and offering his hand. "I'm part of the group that Mr. Wilmot's putting through some kind of adventure training. This is my friend, Ernesto Cardozo, and another of our group, Ms. Lilian Lake."

Bosley took his hand, shook it three times and released. His grip, Ed noticed, was neither too slack, nor too tight.

"Thank you, Mr. Lazenby," he said. "It's nice meeting all of you. Once we get to your camp I'd like to talk to everyone."

"We can talk in the van on the way," Ed said.

"I'd rather talk to each individual in private."

Ed nodded. He understood, and it made sense. That way, he would be able to pick up on any inconsistencies.

"Oh, sure," he said. "That makes sense."

"Why do you travel with a dog?" Lilian asked.

Bosley smiled. "Hercules is trained primarily as a search and rescue animal. If this missing woman, Gertrude Pope, is on the island, he will pick up her scent."

"Even if she's . . . dead?"

"Let's not assume the worse, eh. She could be lost in the woods. Maybe tripped over a root and sprained an ankle or broke a leg. That's how these things usually work out."

Ed hoped that the man was right but was pretty sure he was wrong. He couldn't, explain even to himself, why he was so sure that Gertrude Pope was dead, but his gut told him that was the case, and his gut was usually right. He wouldn't, however, share that thought with any of the others.

"I hope you're right," he said. "If she didn't take any water with her, she'll be pretty dehydrated about now, too. Good thing you brought the dog. Should make finding her easy."

"Once Hercules gets on the scent, he'll take us right to her, eh."

There was something in Bosley's tone that Ed had missed at first, but the way he avoided eye contact with any of them as he spoke about Gertrude's likely condition, he realized that the man probably thought the same thing he did, and was holding back on saying it, probably for the same reasons.

Bosley caught Ed's eye, and in that look an unspoken understanding passed between them. Bosley knew that Ed knew, and he appreciated the way Ed was handling it.

CHAPTER 14

Back at the camp, Bosley commandeered Wilmot's centrally located cabin as the interview site. He started with Wilmot, and was done in less than three minutes, which made sense to Ed since all Wilmot did was call and report that Ed and Lilian had told him that Gertrude was missing.

His interviews with the rest of the group were just as quick. He saved Ed for last.

When Ed was called in, he found Bosley behind a small table, his head in his hands, looking down at a pocket-sized notebook. Hercules sat quietly on the floor at his left. The dog looked up when Ed entered, then turned its attention back to Bosley.

Bosley looked up. "Have a seat, Mr. Lazenby," he said. "I'll try to make this quick."

Ed sat. "Yeah, it's almost eleven. We need to get out looking for Gertrude before it gets dark."

Bosley's brow furrowed. "I'm aware of the urgency, Mr. Lazenby."

Ed held his hands up. "No criticism intended, Trooper Bosley. Just making an observation."

"Sorry, I didn't mean to snap at you, eh. I have a feeling I need you on my side in this."

"Why is that?"

"Let's just say it's a hunch I have. I watched you in the van, the way you dealt with the possibility that Mrs. Pope' already dead, the way you carry yourself. Are you a retired cop?"

"No, I've never been a policeman."

"Your friend, Mr. Cardozo said you've solved a couple of crimes down in DC. Was he pulling my leg?"

"Well, no, I did get accidentally involved in a couple of situations and was helpful to the authorities in solving them."

"He said you were the modest type. I see he was right. So, first, tell me what you know about this, and then I'll tell you what I think. I have a feeling we have a . . . situation here, and I'm gonna need all the help I can get."

"So, you think there was foul play?"

"I can't be sure, but from what Mrs. Lake said, I have to consider the possibility. I mean, what woman takes off without her makeup, right?"

"Yeah, I thought that myself."

"Hey, forget questions, tell me what you think might've happened."

So, Ed told him. He told him about Pope's attitude toward his wife, his suspicions that the man wasn't surprised at her absence, nor did he seem to be unduly upset over it. "The man strikes me as a craven coward, who wouldn't have the guts to do anything himself," Ed said, summing up. "But, I can't help but think that he has something to do with her disappearance. He's not acting like someone whose wife is missing."

"I agree with you on that part," Bosley said. "But, I'm not so sure I agree that he couldn't have done it himself. We don't get many murders here in Maine, about twenty-five percent of the national average, but I've seen otherwise meek people do some horrific things when provoked. A few years ago, for instance, this guy in Chicago stabbed and bludgeoned his mother to death because she wouldn't help him get tickets to a concert."

"I hadn't thought of it quite that way. She did seem to get on his nerves, what with her focus on dressing up, but that hardly seems sufficient motive to kill someone, but then, neither does not getting concert tickets. I guess I've a lot to learn about people."

"Don't we all. Before we get into that, though, I still have to do a search to make certain she didn't just wander off. Want to join me?"

Ed nodded. He'd been skeptical at first, seeing a mere trooper sent to look into the situation, but he was beginning to like the man.

Charles Ray

CHAPTER 15

After concluding the interviews, and before beginning the search, Bosley changed uniforms, donning a short-sleeved blue shirt and slightly darker blue trousers, but still with his Smokey Bear hat, making his attire more appropriate for the humid weather in the forest. Hiss search began in the Pope's cabin. He went over the place inch by inch, paying particular attention to the contents of Gertrude's suitcase. When he was satisfied that the place would yield nothing of use, he took several articles of clothing from her suitcase, and allowed Hercules to get a good whiff of them.

"Now, we'll start at the entrance to this cabin, and then work our way around the perimeter, starting at the entrance road," he said.

"That's to establish whether or not she left, right," Ed said.

Bosley smiled. "Right. Hey, you sure you aren't a retired cop, eh?"

"I am absolutely sure. I just happen to have a logical mind. I listen carefully, and I see connections where other people see nothing. Probably comes from being a systems analyst for the defense department for so long."

"Whatever, you've got a sharp mind, and I think I'm lucky to have you around." He patted Hercules' head. "Okay, boy, let's go find this missing person. Search."

The dog made a 'woof' sound and immediately began sniffing his way to the door. Outside the cabin he began making his way toward the kitchen, but Bosley stopped him with a soft command, 'Stay, boy.' He sat and watched Bosley, waiting for the next command.

"Why'd you stop him?" Ed asked.

"Looks like he was heading for that cabin where you all gather for meals. That would be logical. But, I want to focus on the likely direction she'd take if she was leaving, especially if she was sneaking out, so we'll go directly to the entrance to the site and work our way around the perimeter."

Ed nodded. It made sense. He fell in behind Bosley and Hercules as they headed for the entrance, which was in front of the central cabin, twenty yards away.

Bosley took the dog a few feet beyond the entrance and walked him from one side of the path to the other. Hercules kept his nose to the pebbled surface but didn't seem to find anything interesting. Bosley's face was a study in concentration.

"I don't think he'll find any scent of her there," Ed said. "We got out of the vans near the center cabin, and I don't recall her being anywhere near the entrance."

"I didn't think she would be," Bosley said. "But, it's a good place to start. Now, we'll go around the cabin area clockwise. If she sneaked out, there'll be a scent or some trace of her presence."

Ed noticed that he'd said *if* she sneaked out. What if, he thought, she's still in there somewhere, and we just haven't figured out where to look? He followed Bosley as the trooper directed Hercules in the desired direction.

When they got to the path leading to the training area, Hercules stopped, his tail straight out behind him, his nose near the ground. He growled softly.

"He's got a scent," Bosley said.

"Figured he would here," Ed said. "This is the way we all came and went to the training areas."

"Well, I'll let him follow it anyway. If she sneaked out, she'd probably follow a trail she was familiar with."

Ed nodded even though he didn't agree with Bosley's assessment.

They followed the dog all the way to the training area. Bosley led him around the entire area, but he found no trail leading out besides the one back to the cabins.

"Well, looks like a dead end here," Bosley said. "Just the trail in and out, and there's no place around here to hide that Hercules wouldn't sniff out."

"What about a body?"

Bosley's brows did a little wiggle. "If it was buried really shallow, say four or five inches, maybe, but he's not a cadaver dog. They're specially trained to sniff out decomposing flesh. If she's buried deep, though, Hercules won't get a scent. But, there are no signs of a recent burial here."

"I see that, but I was thinking about some of the other areas. Jason said there are bogs in the deep woods. That strikes me as a good place to hide a body, and from what you just said, unless you know precisely where to look, you might never find it."

"Sadly, that's true. Well, let's do a circle of the cabins staring from here, to see if she took another path out."

They walked until nearly 2:15, and Hercules didn't pick up another scent. Both men were convinced that unless Gertrude Pope left in a vehicle, and the drivers had assured Bosley that the vans never left except to go to the dock to pick him up, she never left the camp.

Had they been trying to 'follow' her trail, Ed knew that there was a chance they might've missed it, but by circumnavigating the entire area, if she left going in any direction, the dog would've hit her scent.

"Well, if she's not somewhere within the camp, she certainly didn't walk out," Ed said.

"Afraid I have to agree with you, Mr. Lazenby. She's either stashed somewhere within the camp, or someone took her out."

"Say, Trooper Bosley, since we're working together, why don't you just call me Ed?"

"Ayuh, okay, Ed, and I'm Nelson."

"What do your friends call you? Do you have a nickname? Any preferences?"

"Anything but late for dinner," Bosley said.

Ed laughed. Who would've thought that the dour-looking cop actually had a sense of humor. "I'll just call you Nelson."

"Works for me."

CHAPTER 16

After arriving back at the cabins, Bosley asked Wilmot to get Pope and bring him for a few more questions. At 3:10, a puzzled-looking Pope entered the cabin. His confused look turned to an angry scowl when he saw Ed sitting beside Bosley at the table they'd put in the center of the room.

"What's he doing here?" he asked, stopping in the open doorway.

"Ed, Mr. Lazenby, is assisting me in this investigation," Bosley said. "Come in, please, and have a seat." He pointed to the empty chair facing him across the table.

"I've already told you all I know. Did you find any sign of my wife?"

The order of his statements, along with the lack of real interest in an answer to his question, was not lost on Ed.

"No," Bosley said. "We found no signs of your wife, now, please have a seat."

Bosley turned the statement into a command with the tone of his voice. He folded his arms across his chest, looking sternly at Pope.

Finally, the older man, sat in the chair, his hands clasped on the table, a truculent look on his face.

"Okay, I'm sitting. What do you want to know?"

Bosley took a small notebook and pen from his shirt pocket and put them on the table.

"First, Mr. Pope, let me say that the evidence we uncovered, or more accurately, failed to find, indicates that your wife never left this camp, at least, she didn't walk out."

Pope slumped in his chair, twiddling his entwined fingers, and stared across the table at Bosley.

"What do you mean, never left the camp? You've looked around. You can clearly see that she's not here."

"I didn't say she was here. I said that she didn't walk away from here. There's a difference."

"I fail to see it." Pope's tone was turning combative.

"What I'm saying, Mr. Pope, is that your wife is *not* here in camp, but she didn't leave of her own free will."

"Wait a minute. You're saying that someone took her away?"

"That's correct. When was the last time you saw or spoke to your wife?"

"Saturday night . . . wait, you don't think I had anything to do with her being missing, do you?"

"I'm not saying anything, sir," Bosley said. "However, to ensure that this conversation is legal, I must advise you of your rights. You have the right to have an attorney present during questioning, and if you cannot afford one, an attorney can be appointed to represent you. You have the right to remain silent, but anything you do say can be held against you in a court of law. Do you understand these rights as I've explained them to you?"

"Hey, I don't know where my wife is, and I swear to you I had nothing to do with her being missing." Pope looked at his hands as he talked.

Ed knew the man was lying, and from the look on his face, so did Bosley.

"I'm not accusing you of anything," Bosley said. "That is a routine question in any missing person case. I will have to fully document what I've learned for the detectives if this turns out to be a criminal matter. Do you understand this?"

"Uh, well, yeah, I suppose so. The last time I saw my wife was Saturday night. We left the kitchen and went back to the cabin. I went out for a smoke—she doesn't like me smoking inside—and when I came back she was already under the covers. I went to sleep. When I woke up yesterday morning, it looked like she was still asleep under the covers, so I went on to the kitchen. That Lake woman is the one who went there and found that she was missing."

Bosley made careful notes in a precise script. When he finished, he looked up at Pope, his expression neutral.

"Do you know of anyone who would want to harm your wife?"

Nah, Gertrude's a doll. Everyone likes her."

Ed knew that the detective was stretching things to allow him to be present, and that the best thing he could do was sit quietly and observe, but he couldn't let Pope's mendacity go unremarked.

"What about the way you ride her all the time?" he said. "Didn't sound like you liked her all that much to me."

Pope looked at Ed and blinked rapidly. Bosley also looked at him, still with that neutral expression. He then looked back at Pope.

"Were you and your wife having problems?" he asked.

Pope glared at Ed. "We argue just like any old married couple," he said. "I suppose to an outsider it would look like we don't like each other very much, and I do criticize my wife for her obsession with dress and makeup, but that's all there is to it."

Charles Ray

Ed knew that was *not* all there was to it but had no concrete evidence to support challenging Pope's statement. He watched Bosley's face. The cop gave no clue to his state of mind, still regarding Bosley with an almost blank expression.

"So, you know of no one who would want to hurt her. Did you have an insurance policy on your wife's life?"

Pope blinked again. Ed smiled. Bosley was pretty good; throwing questions out in a seemingly unrelated fashion to keep the interviewee off balance and possibly get him to make an incriminating statement. Pope, though, wasn't falling for it. He took a deep breath before responding.

"Sure," he said. "We both had policies, each for half a million."

Bosley made another note. "That's a significant sum."

"Not when you consider our situation. I'm a diamond dealer, the sole proprietor of a shop in Bethesda, Maryland. If I die before Gertrude, she's not capable of running the business, so the policy keeps her afloat until it can be sold. She insisted that she have the same policy on her as I had on myself."

"Hm," is all that Bosley said.

"What? You're not trying to imply that I did something to her in order to collect the insurance, are you?"

Bosley looked up, a half-smile on his face. "I'm not implying anything, Mr. Pope, just trying to get as much information as possible. For now, though, I'm upgrading this from a simple missing person case to a possible kidnapping . . . or worse."

There was a flicker of some emotion on Pope's face. Ed wasn't sure, but he thought it might be fear, or guilt, but his usual truculent expression soon replaced it.

76

"I think you're overreacting," Pope said. "I think Gertrude somehow got herself a ride and is holed up, probably back in Bar Harbor in some hotel, hoping I'm miserable wondering where she is."

"We will certainly look into that possibility, Mr. Pope," Bosley said. "That's all I have to ask you for now, but I might have more questions later."

Bosley sat back in the chair, his arms folded across his chest. Finally, realizing that he was being dismissed, Pope stood, shot one last glare at Ed and left, slamming the cabin door behind him.

Ed turned to Bosley. "I don't know, but I got the feeling that he wasn't being totally forthcoming," he said.

Bosley, who had been looking at something in his notebook, closed it and turned to Ed, a serious expression on his face. "If by that you mean he was lying through his teeth, I totally agree," he said.

Charles Ray

CHAPTER 17

Bosley excused himself and went outside to call his headquarters to report what he'd learned so far, and to inform them of his suspicions. He was back in fifteen minutes with a puzzled look on his face.

"What's wrong?" Ed asked. "Didn't your bosses agree with your assessment of the situation?"

"Oh, they agreed all right, and have directed that an investigation be opened."

"That's what you wanted, right?"

"Sure, I wanted a case opened, because it's the right thing to do. But, all the detectives are currently busy on other cases, so the captain has assigned me to deal with it until one of them can be sprung free to come up here."

Ed smiled. "Well, good for you. That must mean your captain has a lot of confidence in you."

Bosley didn't look convinced. "I suppose so, but . . . look, Ed, I haven't been a trooper all that long. In fact, I've only been on the streets for six months. The only reason they sent me on this case was that the other dog handlers were busy, and they thought it'd just be a routine missing person case."

"You could've fooled me, Nelson. You handle yourself like a seasoned officer, and I have no doubt that you'll have this case solved before a detective can arrive."

"Wow, do you think so?"

I'm pretty sure you will. Look, we already have a prime suspect; Harry Pope, and while I don't think he did it himself, I'm convinced he hired someone to do it, and frankly, I think his wife is dead."

"I was sort of coming to that conclusion myself. But, how do we prove any of this?"

"I'm not really sure, but I know that there's only one way to approach it, the way I always approached complex system problems when I worked for the military. You identify all the little pieces of the problem, and then you start putting them together until you have a pretty complete picture."

"Sort of like doing a jigsaw puzzle."

Exactly like a jigsaw puzzle. You go for the easy parts, the corner pieces, or the ones that have an easy to identify symbol or object, and you just keep linking them together."

Bosley shook his head.

"Problem is, I've always been lousy at doing jigsaw puzzles."

CHAPTER 18

Ed suggested that Bosley relocate to his cabin—he assured him that Ernesto was the model of discretion and wouldn't leak details of the investigation, something he wasn't sure he could say about Jason Wilmot—in order to be able to set up a detail board and openly discuss the case. Bosley had, in truth, not been all that comfortable around the tour guide, and readily grabbed his suitcase and Hercules' leash and moved. Ed convinced Wilmot to move a bed from one of the empty cabins into his on a temporary basis, and he'd found an old chalkboard in the corner of the kitchen that had been used on occasion to list the menu for groups using the facility. This, along with a box of multi-colored chalk, he also moved into his cabin, making it quite crowded, something Ernesto remarked upon as soon as he saw it.

"It's a bit cramped, I know," Ed said. "But, we need the privacy so that Nelson can conduct his investigation and maintain confidentiality."

"This mean we can't talk about what goes on in here . . . with anyone?"

"Precisely," Bosley said. "Since one of your fellow campers is our main suspect, we can't risk alerting him to what we know."

"Or don't know," Ed said. "It might come in handy, when he finally realizes that he's under investigation, if he thinks we know more than we do."

"Good point. So, let's get started. What *do* we know?"

Bosley stood at the chalkboard, a piece of white chalk in hand.

"We have the victim, Gertrude Pope," Ed said. "Either missing or dead."

Bosley wrote on the upper left quadrant,

Victim
Gertrude Pope – status, missing or dead?

"Good," he said. "Now, what else do we know? She's been missing since Saturday night or Sunday morning." Ed nodded. "Oh, and there's no sign that she left of her own free will, or at least, Hercules can find no trace of her walking away from the compound."

"Right," Ed said. "We have a principal suspect, the husband, Harry. He and the victim seemed to be at odds."

Bosley wrote,

Suspect
Harry Pope – Husband of victim.
Motive?

He tapped the board. "This is our big problem," he said. "What's his motive? The guy's a diamond dealer, so, despite the insurance policy, I don't think it would be money, and the conflict you and Mrs. Lake described aren't all that uncommon, and don't cross the threshold of what might constitute motive for murder."

"I know." Ed rubbed at his chin. "I can't help but think we're missing something. In the first place, I don't think Pope did anything himself. I think he hired someone."

"Good point." Bosley wrote,

Unknown third party
Hired by husband

"Now, we just have to figure out a way to prove it," he said, tapping the board beneath the new entry.

"I don't suppose there's any way to tell if someone other than our group landed on the island, is there?"

Bosley shook his head.

"You've seen the boat dock. It's unattended, and there are no houses or stores anywhere near it. Besides, there are probably dozens of places on this island where a small boat could land undetected."

Ed shrugged. "Well, that just means we'll have to work harder to solve this case."

Ever the optimist, Ed thought. He stared at the chalkboard, which was beginning to look more and more like a brick wall.

Charles Ray

CHAPTER 19

"Why don't we go to the kitchen and get some coffee," Ed said. "I find that my thought processes work better with caffeine in my system."

"That's just an urban myth," Bosley said. "I don't think caffeine has any effect whatsoever on the cognitive processes. But, I could use a cup just for the comfort right now."

In the kitchen, Rose, Violet, Lilian, and Janet were preparing food. Ed reflected on the fact that the men were all lazing around their cabins, while the women did the 'woman's' work—the notable exception being Bosley and him, who were occupied with trying to solve Gertrude Pope's disappearance. He resolved to have a conversation with Ernesto about that.

"How is the investigation going?" Rose asked when the two men entered the kitchen.

"It's going," Bosley said. "May I get a cup of coffee?"

"My, how polite." Rose pointed at the table. "You sit yourself down, and I'll get you a cup. You like cream and sugar, or black?"

"That's okay, ma'am. I can get my own. You look like you're busy enough as it is."

Ed's respect for the man ratcheted up several notches. Most men would've accepted the offer to fetch for them.

"You go on and have a seat, Nelson," he said. "I'll get coffee for both of us. You like yours black." He said it as a statement, not a question.

"Yes, as a matter of fact, I do," Bosley said. "How did you know?"

"You look like a black coffee man, you know, sort of all business, with a touch of humor now and then."

Bosley laughed. "I don't get the connection, but you're right, I do prefer my coffee black."

"Same as me. I don't like any unnecessary items getting between me and my caffeine."

Ed walked to the counter and filled two cups. Before he could return to the table, Rose moved to his side.

"I take it the investigation is bogged down," she said in a quiet voice.

"Kind of," Ed said.

"What's wrong?"

"Sorry, Rose, but I can't talk about an ongoing investigation."

She followed him back to the table.

"Trooper Bosley, would you tell Ed it's okay to share information with his friends. I, we, would just like to know how your investigation is going."

"I'm sorry, ma'am, but we can't discuss an ongoing investigation with outsiders. It could compromise the integrity of the process."

"Oh, piffle. We're all kind of insiders here under the current circumstances. Now, I imagine you're looking at everyone, with the possible exception of Ed, as potential suspects, but I can assure you that no one presently in this room had anything to do with Gertrude being missing."

"I'm certain of that, ma'am. But still, I can't discuss the details of the investigation with you."

She sat down facing him. "Okay, how about this. I'll say something, and if I'm right, let me know."

"I don't know—"

"Gertrude Pope is missing, and you think she might have been hurt in some way, or even, heaven forbit, killed."

Bosley blinked but said nothing.

"Okay, I'll take that as a yes. Now, you think maybe her husband is involved in her disappearance."

He blinked again.

"I agree. He's a thoroughly disreputable individual. However, I don't believe he actually did anything to her. I think he had someone else do it."

Bosley's mouth fell open. He looked at Ed. "What do you people get up to in that retirement community?"

"Lots of time on our hands," Ed said. "One can only play so many hands of bridge or rounds of golf, so we solve puzzles."

Bosley turned his attention back to Rose.

"Ma'am, I will neither confirm nor deny what you just said, but I would appreciate it if none of that left this room."

She made a sipping motion across her lips. "I am the soul of discretion, just ask Ed. You couldn't make me tell if you threatened to pull out my fingernails. I do, though, know something I think you might find interesting."

"If you know anything that might impact this investigation, I would appreciate hearing it."

She leaned forward and lowered her voice so that only Bosley and Ed could hear. "I was listening to Janet and Lilian talking as we were working, and I heard Janet say that her husband did some work for Harry Pope in the past."

That got both Bosley and Ed's attention.

"Evans didn't say it directly, but he implied that he met the Popes for the first time on this trip," Bosley said. "What kind of work did she say he did for Pope?""

"I didn't hear that part. Maybe you should ask her yourself."

"I'll do that."

He started to rise, but Ed put a hand on his forearm.

CHAPTER 20

"Maybe you should let me ask her," Ed said. "She might respond better to the grandfatherly type."

After a few seconds of thought, Bosley nodded. "You're right. I guess I do come on a bit strong. Find out what her husband does for Pope, and how long he's been doing it. Depending on what she tells you, I'll have some new questions for both Pope and Evans."

"Will do." Ed rose and went to stand beside Janet Evans who was stirring soup in a large pot.

"Hi, Ed," she said, wiping a stray lock of hair from her sweaty brow with her free hand. "I'm making cream of mushroom soup from scratch. Violet showed me how. Isn't that neat?"

"It is, Janet. Could you get someone else to tend it for you for? I need to ask you something, and I'd prefer doing it in private."

She looked around as if worried that someone might have overheard and objected to their conversation. Then, Ed saw something flicker in her eyes.

"Violet," she said. "Could you watch my soup for a few minutes?"

"Sure, Janet," Violet said, given Ed a knowing look. "Take all the time you need."

She wiped her hands on the apron she wore. "Let's go outside," she said. "It should be quiet and private enough there."

Ed followed her outside. She stood with her back to the kitchen cabin, her eyes aimed in the direction of the cabin she shared with her husband.

"I understand," he said. "That your husband works, or worked, for Harry Pope?"

She looked around again, before glancing quickly at Ed. When she finally answered, though, she was still looking at her cabin.

"I don't know if he still works for Mr. Pope," she said. "I wasn't even supposed to know he ever worked for him. Tom's like that, you know. Always telling me that my place is in the kitchen or bedroom, and that I should leave men's business alone."

"Pardon my saying so, Janet, but I think your husband's an ass."

She laughed. Ed thought she was pretty when she laughed.

"No pardon necessary. I *know* he's an ass," she said. "He wasn't like that when we first married, but over time he became more and more domineering and . . . abusive."

"Why do you stay with him?"

"What else can I do? I have a degree in English Lit, and I've been out of school too long to get a decent paying job as a teacher. Besides, I've never worked, and that would be counted against me. Do you have any idea how hard the job market is for a woman my age?"

Ed nodded. "Probably a bit harder than it is for a black man my age," he said. "But, you shouldn't have to put up with the abuse. Have you ever reported him?"

Sadness flickered in her eyes, sadness tinged with fear. "Once, but I couldn't prove it, so the police did nothing, and when they were gone, I got an even worse beating. Tom's become an expert, too, in not leaving obvious bruises."

Feeling his blood pressure rising, Ed decided to change the subject. "Do you know what he did for Pope?"

"Tom's a lawyer. He used to work for a firm that specializes in handling the legal matters of the rich and famous, but then he decided to strike out on his own. He doesn't know that I know this, but his nickname among his lawyer friends is 'The Fixer.'"

"Does that mean what I think it means?"

"I don't know what you think it means, but from what I've overheard when he's on the phone with a client and didn't know I was listening, when some rich guy gets in trouble, like if he gets his mistress pregnant, it's Tom's job to fix it, which I think usually involves the transfer of large sums of money."

"You say usually. What else might it involve?"

"Once I heard him on the phone with someone, and he told this person 'not to leave any marks.' You figure that one out."

Changing the subject hadn't worked. The more he heard about Tom Evans, the more his heart pounded. His cheeks were hot, and he'd clenched his fists so tight, his fingernails were digging into his palms.

"I think I know what it means. Look, Janet, thanks for sharing this with me. It puts a whole new light on things."

"Tom must never know I told you this." There was fear in her voice.

"Don't worry, my lips are sealed. Now, you go on back inside and tend your soup, and tell Trooper Bosley I need to talk to him."

Charles Ray

CHAPTER 21

"A fixer, eh?" Bosley said. "I've heard of lawyers like that. They ought to be disbarred, every flaming one of 'em."

Ed and Bosley were standing at the edge of the parking lot. After he'd told him what he'd learned from Janet Evans, Bosley had slammed a fist into his palm and said, "He's got to be our perp," and then launched into a diatribe about lawyers who use their legal knowledge for less than savory purposes.

"It's unethical as hell, and if Janet's right, some of it's downright illegal," Ed said. "What he needs is to be put in prison where he belongs."

"Darn, but how do we prove it?"

Bosley looked lost.

"Somehow, we have to get him to admit he knew Pope before coming here. I have an idea. It's kind of backward, but it just might work. Why don't we ask Pope?"

"You think he'd answer honestly? The man struck me as a pathological liar."

"True, but if he's not aware of what we're really asking, he might let something slip."

"Jeez, Ed," Bosley said. "I wasn't at the top of my class when they taught interrogation techniques. I mean, I'm okay in a straight-up interview, but what you're talking about here is pretty sophisticated."

Ed shrugged. "Not really. I learned a lot watching the CID guys work when I was at DOD. You want to see if their techniques might work on our friend, Pope?"

"Heck, I don't reckon we have a lot to lose, do we. Let's do it."

They headed for Pope's cabin.

They found him sitting on the vanity chair in front of the cabin, reading a paperback. He didn't appear at all like a man whose wife was missing and presumed dead.

He dog-eared the book, put it on his lap, and frowned up at them as they approached.

"Come back to bother me with more questions, have you?"

"Well, we do have a few follow-up questions we'd like to ask," Bosley said.

"We?" Pope looked from Bosley to Ed, his brow furrowed.

"Mr. Lazenby is helping me, as he is familiar with the surroundings, and he knows all of you."

"Is that even legal?"

"Would you like to consult a lawyer?" Ed asked. "I think, though, he'd tell you that the police are allowed to use consultants."

"Yah, I'll take your word for it. What do you want to ask?"

"You told Trooper Bosley before that you met everyone here in camp for the first time on the ferry," Ed said. "Is that right?"

"Yeah, that's right."

"And, you live in Bethesda?"

"Yeah, I already answered all these questions."

"Sorry," Ed said. "Just establishing that I remember everything correctly. Do you have an attorney to represent you in your jewelry business?"

"Diamond business," Pope said. "I'm not some run of the mill jeweler. I own the biggest diamond export business in the DC area. Of course, I have legal representation. A business like mine without lawyers wouldn't last very long."

"I imagine you use those lawyers on occasion for . . . personal matters as well?"

Pope opened his mouth, then snapped it shut. Bosley smiled, impressed with the way Ed was subtly, and skillfully leading him to the real matter they came to discuss.

Finally, Pope swallowed and glared at Ed. "What do you mean by that?"

"Well, I've heard that a lot of rich, prominent people use their lawyers to, let's say, cover over unpleasant things."

Brows furrowed and eyes narrowed to slits, Pope looked at Ed for a long time, and for just a moment, Ed feared he wouldn't respond to his question. Then, with his jaws tight, Pope spoke. "Are you suggesting that I have a fixer?"

"That's a rather base term. But, I suppose it does describe the kind of duties I was describing. Well, do you?"

"Why in hell would you be asking me that?"

"I'm just curious," Ed said. "Most wealthy people have things that they'd rather never came to light, right? Do you have an attorney on retainer to keep the lid on things?"

"I have no idea what you're talking about."

Ed noticed that he was rather clumsily avoiding a direct answer, giving him a pretty good sign that the answer to his question was 'yes.' He decided to try dropping the courteousness to see what would happen.

"Come on, Harry, don't try to kid a kidder. We happen to know that you in fact *do* have a fixer."

"That's a lie. Sure, I have an attorney, but he handles my business legal affairs, and that's all, and if anyone told you different, he's a freaking liar."

Ed smiled. He'd hit home. Pope's tone was belligerent, but he was sweating.

"Is that a fact? Hm, guess we'll have to go back and ask a few more questions, Trooper Bosley, make sure we got our facts straight."

Without waiting for Pope to react, Ed turned and started walking away. Bosley paused long enough to look down at Pope, His expression was somewhere between pity and scorn. He then turned and caught up with Ed.

"You didn't get much out of him," he said.

Ed shook his head.

"Oh no, I got what I wanted out of him. I never thought he'd own up to Evans being his fixer. What I wanted to do was get a rise out of him, and that I did. Now, we just need to keep an eye on Evans. Dollars to donuts, he and Harry Pope will be having a rather heated conversation within the hour."

Bosley looked confused.

"Look," Ed said. "By accusing him of having a lawyer who fixes things for him, I made him wonder where we got the information. It couldn't be his wife, since she's missing, and I doubt if he knows that Evans' wife knows about their arrangement. So, that leaves Tom Evans as our source. What you wanta bet he'll confront him about it?"

Bosley's eyes widened and he smiled.

"Why, you devious son of a gun. I would never have thought to do that. In fact, I don't remember that being one of the techniques they taught us at the academy."

"In that case, that puts you one up on your colleagues, my boy. Just think what a detective you'll be with that skill in your toolbox."

As they walked back toward the kitchen, there was a bit of swagger in Bosley's step, and a wide smile on his face.

Charles Ray

CHAPTER 22

It didn't take an hour for Pope to confront Evans. It was more like fifteen minutes. Ed and Bosley had grabbed themselves cups of coffee and two chairs and were sitting outside the kitchen cabin so they could see down the line of cabins and see who came and went, and fifteen minutes after they'd departed Pope's place, he came storming out and headed straight for Evans' cabin.

He rapped so loudly on the door, even several buildings away they could hear the thud of his fists on the wood.

The door opened and Evans, his hair mussed, stood there, barefoot and with his tee shirt hanging out of his pants. Pope began waving his hands and clenching his fists and saying something in a low voice that didn't' carry to the kitchen. Evans looked puzzled and was shaking his head.

After a few more minutes of a heated, mostly one-way conversation, Pope poked Evans in the chest, turned and stomped back to his cabin. Evans stood in front of his cabin watching him leave, shaking his head.

"Well," Bosley said. "You were right. What do we do now?"

"Let Evans stew a bit wondering who told us about their relationship, and then we go have a little chat with him."

"Are you thinking what I'm thinking?"

"That Pope paid Evans to arrange for his wife to disappear? Yeah, that's what I'm thinking. I imagine he got Evans to hire some goons to do it. Thinking about it, Pope doesn't strike me as the type to get his hands dirty if he can pay someone else to do it."

"Good point," Bosley said. "Now, all we have to do is prove it. It'd help if we had a body."

"Let me think on that a few minutes," Ed said. "Maybe we can use what we know about Evans and Pope to get him to lead us to the body, or at least give us a hint where to look. You don't mind my taking the lead on this, do you?"

"So far, you've been batting a thousand. My captain wouldn't like me letting a civilian get so involved in a case, but my captain's not here, so I'm making a command decision. Until I say so, you're running interrogations . . . partner."

They shook hands and went back their coffee. A germ of an idea began to sprout in Ed's mind.

Ed waited until about an hour before supper, figuring this had given Evans enough time to stew over whatever Pope had said to him. With Bosley in tow, he made his way to Evans' cabin.

He'd brushed his hair and put on a shirt but was still barefoot when he answered their knock. He frowned when he saw them.

"What do you want? I've already told you everything I know," he said, and started to step back and close the door.

Ed put his foot in, blocking him.

"Trooper Bosley has a few more questions for clarification," he said. "You mind stepping outside? I'm sure you'll prefer he ask those questions in private."

Evans looked over his shoulder. "Don't matter, you can come in," he said. "Janet's at the kitchen helping those other old biddies fix supper."

They pushed in past him.

The place was messy, or at least, half messy. The side farthest from the door was neat, bed made and clothing folded neatly on a chair, while the near side looked like a teenager's room, with socks, underwear, and rumpled jeans scattered near the unmade bed.

Evans crossed the room, dumped the clothing from the chair, and brought it around.

"Only got the one chair," he said. "You guys can draw straws for it."

"That's okay, I can stand," Ed said.

"Yeah, we won't be long," Bosley added.

"Suit yourself." Evans plopped down on the end of the bed. "What do you want?"

"For starters, why did you mislead us about your relationship with Harry Pope?" Bosley's tone was deliberately accusatory.

Evans looked down at the floor.

"I didn't mislead you," he said.

"You didn't tell us that you are his lawyer."

He looked up.

"You never asked me if he was."

Bosley looked at Ed. Ed stepped forward.

"You and Harry Pope have been acting like you never met before, even on the ferry," Ed said. "And, it was whether or not you knew him before coming here that Trooper Bosley is referring to. The fact that you're his legal representative only makes your concealment of the relationship the more curious, and, I might add, suspicious."

Evans looked from Ed to Bosley. Bosley looked at Ed and nodded.

"Hey, detective, old Ed here's no cop," Evans said. "He doesn't have the right to question me."

"Technically, he didn't ask a question, he made a statement," Bosley said. "And, for your information, he is consulting on this case, and I've given him the authority to ask questions. So, here's a question, why didn't you tell me you knew the Pope's before?"

"Uh, you never asked that specific question, and it didn't seem relevant."

Bosley turned to Ed. "He says he didn't think it was relevant. In light of what we've learned, what's your take on that?"

"I think Mr. Evans didn't want us to know that he knew the Popes before coming here. What I don't know is why he'd be reluctant for that to be known."

He turned back to Evans.

"You see my problem, Mr. Evans," he said. "As my colleague says, it appears that you deliberately concealed information that's material to my investigation. Now, I'd be interested in knowing why you did that, and don't give me that 'I didn't think it was relevant,' bull. We're trying to find out what happened to Gertrude Pope, and knowing them, you might know something that would help us do that."

"Uh, I didn't know Gertrude," Evans said. "When I met her on the ferry in Bar Harbor, it was the first time I'd ever laid eyes on her, and that's the truth."

"What about George Pope? Was Bar Harbor the first time you saw him?" Ed asked.

"And, be careful how you answer that question, Mr. Evans," Bosley said. "You see, we already know the answer, so if you lie . . . well, let's just say it's best if you tell the truth."

Evans looked from Ed to Bosley and back to Ed. Indecision was written all over his face, and his brow was shiny and slick with sweat. Finally, he signed.

"Okay, so I know George Pope. There's nothing untoward in that."

"You do certain jobs for him, right?"

"I do a lot of his legal work, yes."

"No," Ed said. "What he means is that you handle other sensitive matters for him."

"I don't know what you mean."

"Oh, I think you do, Tom. I think you handle certain sensitive matters for Harry Pope, things he doesn't want bandied about in public."

Evans blinked. Between him and Pope, Ed thought, there'd been a lot of blinking. Both men displayed the same indicators of lying. Or, in Evans case, preparing to lie.

"Hey, I refuse to dignify such a statement with a response," he said.

"Why would you not want to answer a simple question? It sounds simple enough to me," Bosley said.

"I know my rights. I don't have to answer any of your questions."

"True, and if you were a suspect, I would have to inform you of our Miranda rights. Do I need to do that?"

A brief flare of panic flashed in Evans' eyes, but he quickly regained control.

"No, there's no need for that. I haven't done anything illegal. But, I can't discuss what goes on between my client and me; attorney-client privilege, and all that. You understand."

"Sure, I understand. Your client doesn't want his dirty linen washed in public, so he uses you to do the laundry."

"That's a slanderous statement about my client and about me. I could report you to the authorities, you know."

Bosley laughed. "Please do, and don't forget to tell them exactly what I said. In order to prove slander, you have to show that I was wrong about what I said. Or will you also refuse to answer them when they ask if you work as a fixer for Harry Pope."

Evans' face had gone pale.

"Don't answer that," Bosley said. "I think we learned what we came to learn. By the way, we have some leads on where we might find Gertrude Pope. I'm having a special search team come out tomorrow morning to confirm what I suspect. Oh, and by the way; Harry Pope's been almost as uncooperative as you, but he's beginning to crack. I doubt if he'll go down by himself, know what I mean?"

Evans tried to keep his expression neutral, but Ed saw another flicker of fear in his eyes.

"We'll talk more tomorrow, Mr. Evans. Come on, Ed. You can buy me a cup of coffee."

CHAPTER 23

After leaving Evans' cabin, Ed and Bosley watched from the parking lot, sitting on the grass that lined in on the right, behind a large bush. They took turns getting food, coffee, and going to the latrine. It was Ed's first stake out, and he found it boring. Bosley took it like the stoic New Englander, or as he said it, like a Down-Easter, which was what residents of Maine called the area where Bar Harbor is located.

"Winters down east are long, so you learn to sit and enjoy the quiet," he said, when Ed asked him how he could sit still so long without fidgeting.

So, until just before midnight, they sat and enjoyed the quiet. After a while, Ed actually found it relaxing. There was something about sitting under in the dark without pollution or city light obscuring the stars, listening to the chirping night creatures, and far off, the crashing of the surf on the rocky beach that was soothing. For a moment, Ed didn't miss the constant din of traffic on Georgia Avenue a few blocks away from the main entrance to PVC, or the background hum of electricity through miles of wire, feeding hundreds of hungry appliances that themselves made a subliminal noise that you aren't aware of until you're in a place without them.

Even in the early weeks of summer, the first week in June, there was a pleasant nip in the night air, which bore the salty tang of the sea, instead of the hydrocarbon-laden, swamp-moist air he had to breathe in the Washington, DC area.

He leaned back, and though he looked often at Evans' cabin, he also gazed up at the inky black sky festooned with the twinkling points of uncountable stars.

"I can see why people like living in a place like this," he said.

"Ayah," Bosley said. "You don't get to see a beautiful sky like this when you live in a city." He, too, was alternating his gaze between the cabin and the sky. "Makes you realize just how insignificant we humans are, doesn't it?"

Ed could only nod, a gesture that Bosley didn't see, but which didn't, as it normally would have, bother Ed. He was beginning to understand the phlegmatic nature of New Englanders, at least the rural ones. They had no need for gestures.

Then, just as he looked back at the cabin, he saw at first a slit of light that got wider as Evans opened the door. His body was a dark shape against the light as he stepped outside, and then, for a moment, it disappeared into the darkness as he closed the door.

"Looks like he's on the move," Ed said.

Bosley put a hand on Ed's shoulder. "Dang, how'd you know he'd do something like this?"

Ed chuckled. "By planting the seed in his mind that maybe we know more than we do, and bringing Pope's name into it, had to set him to wondering. I'll bet you he told Pope what he did, and maybe even where he put the body." By now, Ed was convinced that Evans had killed Gertrude Pope and stashed her body somewhere, rather than bring in outsiders to do it. "He has to be worried that Pope will eventually spill his guts, if indeed he hasn't already done so."

They watched as Evans moved around away from the cabin and flicked on a penlight.

"Well, with that light, he'll at least be easy to follow."

They waited until he was just about to enter the trail to the training area, and then started following.

He was walking faster than Ed had expected, though, and by the time they reached the entrance to the trail, he was no longer in sight.

"Dagnabit," he said. "I don't see him now."

"So, what do we do?"

"We could stumble around in the dark, and maybe alert him he's being followed," Ed said. "Or, we could wait here for him to come back and see if we can figure out where he went. That'll give us a place to start searching for a body."

Bosley agreed that Ed's plan was the wisest course, and they found a place in some bushes near the entrance, and sat back, again switching between watching the trail and contemplating the stars.

It was nearing dawn, and they were both getting drowsy when they heard the sound of someone come through the bushes from the forest that lined the trail to the training area. After a few minutes, Evans, his pants shiny with mud, stepped from the undergrowth. He looked around, and then walked quickly back toward his cabin.

"He was gone a long time," Bosley said. "It's gonna be difficult to narrow down a place to search."

"Not really," Ed said. "I think I know where he's been."

Charles Ray

CHAPTER 24

After being assured by Bosley that the state's specially trained cadaver dog could detect a corpse under up to 15 feet or more of water, Ed told him to ask for that team and the equipment to dig in a bog, where he was sure they would find Gertrude Pope's body.

"How do you know?" Bosley asked.

"That mud on Evans' trousers," Ed replied. "It was kind of blue-gray, and I remember an area near where we did the zip line exercise had boggy ground with a bluish-gray clay composition. His pants were still wet and shiny, which means he likely was there last. I think he moved the body from wherever he originally stashed it to there."

"Hm, makes sense. Okay, I'll call it in."

Bosley called his headquarters and outlined Ed's request—without mentioning Ed, as he hadn't told his bosses that he was making use of Ed's expertise. He was told to expect the cadaver dog team and a team with a backhoe by three in the afternoon.

"Guess there's nothing to do now but wait," Ed said, after Bosley broke the phone connection. "It's too late to go to sleep. Besides, I never sleep well in daytime. We might as well have breakfast and get ourselves comfortable. Let Evans think he's gotten away with something for now."

"I suppose you're right." Bosley made a huffing sound. "But, letting him roam free, knowing that he's probably a murderer, just doesn't sit right with me."

"Don't worry, Nelson, you'll get him. It's not like he has anywhere he can go. What was it you said to me last night about being patient?"

"Yeah, yeah, I know. Okay, breakfast sounds like a good idea. I'm starved."

After breakfast, Jason Wilmot gathered everyone in front of his cabin, Bosley included.

"Trooper Bosley," Wilmot said. "Can we resume our normal activities now?"

Bosley looked at Ed, who nodded slightly.

"I suppose so," Bosley said. "In fact, it's not a bad idea to keep everyone together. You mind if I join in?"

"Not at all."

They marched off to the training area.

Once there, Wilmot had them go through an obstacle course, similar to what Ed remembered from his army basic training. He was not surprised that Bosley, such a recent police academy graduate, and younger than everyone except Janet Evans and Wilmot, outperformed everyone. Ed, surprisingly, was able to keep up with the young cop, only just, but he didn't push himself too hard, saving some of his energy to watch Pope and Evans. He noticed that the two men studiously avoided each other, and whenever they were forced into close proximity traded glares. Each time it happened, he smiled. His stirring of the pot had caused a schism between them, and he knew it was just a matter of time until it would be a full-blown breakup.

Back at the cabins for lunch, everyone, again but for Pope and Evans, both of whom stalked off to their cabins as soon as they got back, sat around in front of

Wilmot's cabin and talked about the morning's exercise.

"So, Ed," Lilian said. "They made you do things like that when you were in the army?"

"Yeah, they did, and you know something funny? I'm not as fast as I was back then, but I didn't trip and fall as many times as I did then, either."

"You did a great job, considering," Wilmot said.

"Considering that I'm an old man?"

"I didn't mean it like that." The tour guide's cheeks turned red.

"Yes, you did," Ed said. He laughed. "But, that's okay. I know I'm old, and I'm proud of it. Better to be old than the alternative."

"I hear that," Ernesto said.

"You didn't do so bad, yourself, Ernesto," Rose said.

"I got a lot of experience running, ducking and dodging as a mail man," he said. "There were at least six dogs on my route, and each of them wanted a bite out of the postman. I serviced that route for ten years and was never once bitten."

"That's quite an achievement," Bosley said. "You know, you guys are in good shape. My dad's about your age, and he just sits around in his rocking chair watching *Fox News* and fussing about the liberals that are taking the country to hell, and he's shrinking every day. I wish I could get him to come on a trip like this."

"You should first throw his TV away so he can't watch the news," Violet said. "That's what's causing him to shrink, because it's slowly rotting his brain."

Bosley shrugged.

"What about your mom," Ed said. "Can't she get him to exercise>"

"My mom died fifteen years ago. It's been just me and dad since, and I don't have the hart to push him too hard."

"You'd be doing him a favor. People our age need to be active, or we wither and die. Sometimes a little tough love is called for."

"Dang, you're right. I'm gonna pull him off that couch as soon as I get back home. Maybe I'll start slow, like making him take a walk with me."

Ed was about to say that what he planned was a good idea, but he shouldn't expect miracles, when the sound of the ferry horn echoed off the walls of the cabins.

"Sounds like the ferry's here," he said. "Let's go meet your people."

"What people?" Wilmot asked.

Ed looked at Bosley.

"Might as well tell them now," he said. "They'll know soon enough anyway."

Bosley nodded.

"You're right. Look, folks," he said. "I'm afraid that evidence indicates that Gertrude Pope is probably dead, and her body's somewhere on this island. Ed and I think we know the general area, so I've asked that a cadaver dog team and some digging equipment be sent out. That should be them coming in on the ferry now."

"Digging equipment," Lilian said. "Does that mean you think she's buried somewhere? Then, that would mean—"

"Yes, ma'am, it would mean a strong possibility of foul play. Now, Ed and I are going to the pier to meet them. I would ask that the rest of you remain here near the cabins until further notice."

Without waiting for a response from anyone, he nodded at Ed to follow him, and they headed for the parking lot.

A buzz of conversation started immediately, with speculations about what might have happened to Gertrude flying around like confetti at a Mardi Gras parade.

CHAPTER 25

The cadaver dog, a female German shepherd named Penelope, looked like Hercules' twin. Her handler, a state police sergeant named Lawrence O'Shea, was a dour man, probably, Ed surmised, due to the nature of his work. Along with O'Shea came Darla Johnson, a forensic technician whose job would be to process the scene if a body was found, and Duncan Watson, a bald, brown skinned man who operated the backhoe, which had been lashed to the deck of the ferry and took nearly twenty minutes to unload.

Bosley greeted them as they came off the ferry and introduced Ed as someone who could guide them to a likely search area. Ed noticed that he made no mention of allowing him to participate in the investigation.

After all gear had been taken off the ferry, and items not needed for the immediate search, which included the backhoe, secured in Ed's cabin, they set out.

The area he thought might contain Gertrude's body was a marshy area just south of the zip line terminus. Wilmot had pointed it out the first day and warned them to stay away from it, and especially not to go in alone, because a lone traveler getting mired in such a place ran the risk of not being found for days because of the dense undergrowth, and the fact that cries for help in the thick woods might not be heard in the training area. A good place to hide a body, Ed thought, and wondered why Evans hadn't put the body there in the first place; just one of the many question he would have to ask, or have Bosley ask, if they indeed found a body.

When they arrived at the site, an area of some two hundred square meters or more, Ed pointed out to them the distinctive blue-gray color of the clay. Bosley agreed that was the color of the mud spatter on Evans' trousers. Sergeant O'Shea than ordered them to stand back out of the way and let Penelope do her thing.

Ed found it fascinating to watch O'Shea and Penelope work. They started at one corner of what O'Shea called 'the grid', and, like mowing a lawn or plowing a field, did a back and forth sweep, with Penelope's nose to the surface of the ground, and at small pools of water, she would actually lap up some, which O'Shea explained, when Ed gasped, helped in the location of a corpse in water.

Ed hadn't understood much of O'Shea's explanation of how that was done; something about corpses releasing certain chemicals into the air, water and soil that Jacobson's Organ, a sensory trigger in dogs, could collect. Trained to respond to the presence of these chemicals, the dogs would alert their handlers as Penelope was doing now. O'Shea had gone on at some length on the subject, using terms Ed didn't understand, until he finally shut his mind to the man's endless droning and concentrated on watching the dog work. Bosley seemed convinced that Penelope would find Gertrude's body if it was there, even if it was under 40 feet of water, a claim Ed found hard to believe, but there were no other options for finding the missing woman, so he kept his doubts to himself.

Which, it turned out, was a good thing, because, at a spot near the middle of O'Shea's invisible 'grid', Penelope made a 'whuff' sound, and sat. O'Shea turned toward them.

"She found something," he said.

The spot he pointed at was not under water as such, but the ground was wet and shiny from a thin film of water, there being so much water under the surface it couldn't be absorbed. This made the ground liquid, which meant any signs of digging would've long since disappeared, but O'Shea looked confident, as did Bosley.

Bosley turned to the forensic specialist.

"What do you think, Darla," he said. "Can we bring in the backhoe now?"

She pushed a stray lock of dark brown hair away from her brow.

"Sure, just let me get some crime scene tape up first," she said. "I'll leave an opening for the backhoe."

Watson, the backhoe operator, turned and started back toward the cabins. "I'll go get Betsy," he said over his shoulder.

Ed looked at Bosley. "He calls his backhoe, Betsy?"

Bosley shrugged. "Men and their machines."

Within five minutes, Watson was back, sitting in the plexiglass-enclosed cab of a machine that looked like a dinosaur constructed with Lego™ blocks. The cab, a metal and plexiglass box, sat atop huge treads. Protruding from the front was a two-part articulated boom with an inverted toothed-bucket at the end. If Ed had been skeptical about a dog finding a body under water, he was in total disbelief that this ungainly contraption would be able to retrieve that body, but he'd been proven wrong about the dog, so he kept his comments about this being the wrong way to go about it to himself. If it had been his decision, he would've brought in several workers with shovels and, like an archaeologist at an ancient site, begun to remove the earth a few inches at a time.

As Watson maneuvered the backhoe and positioned the bucket to begin his first scoop, Ed realized that this method, as much as it resembled swatting mosquitos with a baseball bat, at least saved time.

Then, Watson amazed him. He positioned the teeth of the bucket, dropped it, penetrating the ground about six inches, and then slowly, drew the bucket backwards, the motion that gives the machine its name, scooping up six inches of dirt, muck, vegetation, and water. He then swiveled the bucket and dumped its contents at a spot indicated by Darla Johnson. It was all done with such finesse, Ed began to reassess his attitude. Clearly, Watson was a virtuoso with this machine, and experienced at such operations. Beside him, Bosley, Ed noticed, was smiling his approval.

"He seems to know what he's doing," Ed said.

"Duncan's been runnin' that backhoe for ten years," Bosley said. "He's so good, he can scoop up s dime and hardly disturb the ground."

Ed doubted that, but there was no doubt that Watson knew what he was doing.

"The thing is, though, at the pace he's going, unless the body isn't buried deep, it'll be dark before he finds anything."

Bosley pointed to an olive drab box strapped to the back of the backhoe.

"Won't matter," he said. "Duncan brought his portable floodlights. He'll keep working even after dark. If there's a body there, he'll find it."

Ed was impressed. These people were pros, he thought, who had planned for every contingency. He was beginning to feel more positive. But, there was still the waiting, and now it was worse than the stakeout in the parking lot, because it could lead to a real break in the investigation. He watched Bosley, who stood impassively watching the backhoe's bucket carefully scooping a few inches of slimy earth and depositing it, where Johnson, her white jumpsuit now a slimy blue, knelt and felt around carefully.

There was nothing to say, so Ed took his cue from Bosley and stood patiently, or as patiently as he could manage, and watched the process unfold.

It started getting dark around 6:30, so Duncan stopped the backhoe and set up the lights. Under the eerie glow of four flood lamps, he resumed his methodical excavation.

Ed glanced at his watch every few minutes, willing the bucket to come up with something each time. After what seemed like an eternity, he glanced down to see the green numerals 10:45, and took a deep breath. He'd missed supper, and his back and legs were sore from standing on one place so long. His stomach growled, and he realized that they hadn't planned for *every* contingency. No one had thought to bring food.

Just as he was about to point that out to Bosley, Johnson shouted, "Hold it, Duncan, I see something that looks like a cloth fragment in the bucket."

Ed and Bosley started forward, but Johnson waved them back. "Wait until I've had a chance to check it," she said. "If it's a body, I want to make sure you guys don't contaminate the scene."

The bucket was lowered slowly until it was level with her waist. She leaned forward, peering in, and then began manipulating things with her hands. After a few seconds, she straightened and turned.

"It's a body all right. Female, Caucasian, and looks like she's been strangled. You can come take a look."

They moved to her side. Ed almost heaved when he saw what was left of Gertrude Pope. He'd seen dead bodies before, including the mutilated corpses of comrades who'd run into VC booby traps in Vietnam, but this wasn't a war zone, and he'd never seen a body that hadn't been prepared by a mortician outside a war zone.

The body had been in the ground less than three days, but the water and the bacteria that lived in the wet soil had already started doing their work. A body goes through several stages of decomposition beginning immediately after death. As soon as the heart stops beating, the body starts heating or cooling to match its environment, in a process called *algor mortis*. With three to six hours, the muscles become rigid. This is known as *rigor mortis*, and because the heart's no longer pumping blood, that blood remaining in the body is pulled by gravity to the lowest point; a process known as lividity, which results in discoloration in the parts to which the blood drains. Other than this and occasionally blisters from the breakdown of cells and tissues from the lack of oxygen being moved through the body, there are few other physically apparent changes. It is during the second phase of decomposition that the most gruesome changes occur, exacerbated when a body has been placed in a wet environment. The accumulation of gases in the body causes it to bloat, and the gases produced, mainly hydrogen sulfide, carbon dioxide, methane and nitrogen, cause the natural fluids and the liquefying tissues to become frothy. Sometimes this buildup of internal gases causes a body to rupture, and it takes on an overall grayish, marbled appearance.

That was the sight that greeted Ed when he looked into the backhoe's bucket. Her face had bloated almost beyond recognition, but Ed recognized the clothing Gertrude had been wearing the last time he'd seen her on Saturday evening during supper.

He also saw why Johnson believed that she'd been strangled. Her tongue was sticking out between her grossly swollen lips, and the scarf she'd worn draped over her shoulders was still knotted tightly around her swollen neck.

The smell of the beginning of putrefaction, now that the body was exposed to air, was strong, and Ed had to fight back the urge to vomit. He held his hand over his nose, but it did little to keep the stench out. He wondered how Bosley, Johnson, and Watson could be so calm. He resolved, though, to emulate them.

"You're right," he said. "Looks like someone strangled her with her own scarf."

"You recognize it?" Bosley asked.

"Yeah, the clothing, too. It's what she was wearing at supper Saturday night."

"So," Johnson said. "You feel certain this is Gertrude Pope, the missing woman?"

Ed nodded. "Yeah, I'm almost one hundred percent sure this is her. Even with the disfigurement of the face, it looks like her, and those are definitely the clothes she was wearing when I last saw her."

The forensic tech nodded. "Okay, then. I'll note it in my report as most likely Gertrude Pope. Of course, when they do the autopsy, they'll do DNA and dental records to make sure. Anyway, Nelson, you've got yourself a homicide here."

"Speaking of that," Bosley said. "Other than she was strangled, what can you tell me?"

"Strange thing for someone strangled with a scarf. Usually that's done from behind. From the way the knot's positioned, though, I'd say she was strangled by someone standing directly in front of her."

"Hm, in order to get close enough to do that, it would have to be someone she knew and was comfortable allowing into her personal space."

Johnson lifted one of the corpse's hands in her gloved hand. "True, but from the condition of her nails, and I can't be sure how much of this might not be attributable to being buried in this muck, she put up a good struggle."

Ed looked closely and saw that several of the nails were broken off at the tip.

"I remember she had those pointy fingernails that seem to be so popular. If they broke off in a struggle, wouldn't the other person have some scratches?"

"Probably," Johnson said. "Depends, though. If he was wearing a heavy shirt he might not have gotten any skin damage."

"You're assuming she was killed by a man?" Ed asked.

"Yes. Strangling like this is not typically a woman's crime. Besides, the strength required to do this would mean a pretty big woman."

Ed thought of Violet, who was tall, and strong, but, of course, she wouldn't kill anyone—except with her sharp, often vindictive tongue.

"I see what you mean." He nodded. "Well, Nelson, we have a suspect, and now we have a body. What's our next step?"

Johnson looked from Ed to Bosley, her brows raised.

"Ed, Mr. Lazenby, was, er, is helping me, okay," he said.

"Hey, I'm not criticizing," Johnson said. "I know what it's like to be shorthanded. Do you see any other techs on this scene right now? If Ed wants to help me, I'll deputize him in a heartbeat."

"No thanks," Ed said. "I'm not very good around dead bodies."

"You're better than most," she said. "Most of the rookie cops faint at their first sight of a corpse, and that's in the sterile environment of the morgue. You held it in like a pro under some pretty adverse conditions."

If Ed's complexion had been any lighter, they would've seen him blush. Instead, he simply ducked his head in acknowledgment of her compliment.

"Okay," Bosley said. "Let's get this crime scene secure, get the remains prepared for transfer to the lab, and Ed, you and I have a couple of conversations to have. It's not gonna be easy, though. These two guys are practiced liars."

"I have an idea," Ed said. "But, first, Ms. Johnson, I need to know something."

"What?"

"Would any trace of the killer be left on a body that's been buried in this muck for as long as this one has?"

"If you mean fingerprints, I doubt it. If she scratched him and broke the skin, we might find something, but the water will have washed most of that away. Same with the scarf. If it had been kept dry, the killer might've sweated on it and left enough DNA trace for ID, but it's been submerged in this mud, so that's probably washed away as well."

"But, under ideal circumstances, there must might be some trace of the killer on the body?"

"Sure. Strangling is a very personal crime, and when you make that kind of physical contact, it's almost inevitable you'll leave some trace. Why do you ask?"

"Well," he said. "I didn't know any of this until just now. I'm betting that the same thing goes for Evans and Pope."

It took Bosley a few seconds, but then the lights came on in his brain.

"I see. That just might work," he said. "Ed Lazenby, you are one devious person, you know that?"

"Hey, you work in the Pentagon as long as I did, it rubs off on you."

CHAPTER 26

The temperature in Ed's cabin wasn't that high, but Tom Evans was sweating.

He'd put on a good front when Bosley summoned him, arriving with the usual belligerent expression on his face, but when the trooper told him that they'd found Gertrude Pope's body, his demeanor underwent a subtle transformation. He still maintained the 'look down your nose' sneer, but his eyes wouldn't stay aimed in one direction for long, and beads of sweat appeared on his forehead.

"That's terrible," he said. "She was buried near the area where we did the zip line exercise, you say?"

His attempt to put a tone of sympathy and shock in his voice was so blatantly lame, Ed had to bite his bottom lip to keep from laughing aloud.

"Yes," he said. "Or more accurately, she was re-buried there. Originally she was buried deeper in the woods."

A muscle in Evans' cheek quivered.

"How do you know that?"

"We have our ways," Bosley said. "We have a few more questions for you, Mr. Evans, about your relationship with Mr. and Mrs. Pope."

"Look, I already told you that I do some minor legal work for Harry Pope. Why do you keep harping on that?"

"Let's just say that finding Mrs. Pope's body kind of puts a different light on things. Now, I'm forced to wonder why you chose to conceal the fact that the two of you were previously acquainted."

Evans had the expression of a rabbit that has been driven into a corner by a hungry fox. He knew he was about to be eaten. But, like a rabbit, that will fight when cornered, even though that fight can only end one way, he came out swinging.

"My decision not to share that information is none of your business. As a lawyer, my client's confidentiality is all important. So, I don't usually go around advertising the relationship, so what. It's not a crime."

"No, it's not," Ed said. "But, it could be done to cover up a crime."

"What the hell does that mean?"

"According to Harry Pope, whenever he has a particularly complex or nasty job, you're his go-to guy. Apparently, in his opinion the attorney-client privilege only protects in one direction."

Some of the fight went out of Evans' expression. He now looked like the rabbit that's just about resigned to being eaten.

"Harry wouldn't do a thing like that," he said, but there was no conviction in his voice.

"You would be surprised at what a man will do when he's looking at life in prison," Bosley said. "Then again, as a lawyer, you shouldn't be surprised."

Ed smiled. He faced Evans fully when he did, a wolfish grin that said, 'gotcha.'

"Uh, I'm not a trial lawyer," Evans said. "I know about plea bargains, but I've never done a criminal case."

"Well," Ed said. "You'd better brush up on your criminal law, because I think you're gonna need it . . . and, a good lawyer for yourself."

"Wha-, why in hell should I need a lawyer? I've done nothing but conceal a relationship with a client. That he might be guilty of some crime, well, as I said, I don't do criminal cases, but as his attorney of record, I'll see that he gets the best criminal defense lawyer his money can buy."

"So, now he's such a good client, you're going to help him defend himself," Bosley said. "But, who's going to help defend you?"

"I ask again, why should I need a lawyer?"

Ed looked at Bosley. Bosley smiled, bowed, and said, "Would you like to do the honors, Ed?"

Ed returned the bow. "I would be delighted. Mr. Evans, Mr. Pope is maintaining that you are the one who killed his wife, that you tried to seduce her, and when she refused you, you killed her in a fit of rage."

He was, of course, making all this up, basing it on what he knew about Evans and his attitudes toward women.

"He wouldn't do that?" Evans protested.

"Like I already said." Bosley was still smiling. "Faced with life in jail, people do all kinds of things. Maybe he's looking for a reduced sentence. According to Ed here, and I imagine others here would back him up, you have on at least one occasion threatened violence toward a woman not your wife, and you are regularly abusive, probably physically, toward her. That, along with the physical evidence linking you to the deceased should be a slam dunk for even one of our newly-assigned prosecutors."

Evans smiled. "There can't be any evidence linking me to Gertrude. You said she was buried in wet dirt. That would've washed off any physical evidence."

"You got it wrong, sir," Bosley said. "That applies when the body is completely submerged in water, primarily sea water. But the surrounding earth, even wet, muddy clay, helps to insulate the remains from the water, preserving a good bit of the DNA traces that I'm sure the ME will find."

Evans' face lost all color. Bosley smiled.

"You really shouldn't have left that scarf around her neck," he said. "The force you had to apply to strangle her with that will undoubtedly left your DNA on it, and the mud will have preserved it quite well."

Ed had always thought the images he'd read about of people actually seeming to shrink were just that, literary images from the mind of the author, but he watched as Evans shrank before his eyes. The man seemed to be slowly deflating like one of those air-filled things you see at used car lots with a pinhole in it, slowly collapsing.

Evans looked down at his bare feet. He looked up, first at Ed, then at Bosley.

"It wasn't my idea," he said. "Harry made me do it. He said he'd turn me in to the bar association for some of the things I've done for him, claiming that I did them without his consent or authorization. They'd know he was lying, but I'd still probably be disbarred just for doing them, even with his authorization."

"So," Bosley said. "You admit to killing Gertrude Pope, and claim that her husband asked you to do it? What was his reason for wanting her dead?"

"He's been wanting to expand his diamond business, but despite her love of finery, Gertrude developed a conscience and wanted him to divest himself of diamonds and go into something else, because so many of the diamonds he's been acquiring are probably blood diamonds. Hell, I'm pretty sure they *are* blood diamonds because he gets them at a cheaper price than the ones bought on the regular market. Anyway, he dug in his heels, and so did she. She wouldn't let him do it."

"How could she do that?" Ed asked.

"Hah, because, the money that helped Ed start his business in the first place came from her. She inherited millions from her parents when they died. She's been bankrolling him from the start. Hell, that's why he married her in the first place. Anyway, he figured with her out of the way, he could do as he pleases since he'll inherit everything."

Bosley looked at Ed, an expression of distaste.

"It had to be either another woman, or money," Ed said. "Those are the two main reasons for someone to want a spouse dead. This is the first time, though, I've ever heard of someone using his lawyer to do it."

"That's it," Evans said. "He used me. Look, whatever deal that bastard made with you, I'll better it. I can not only finger him for ordering the murder of his wife, but I know every crooked diamond deal he's done over the past ten years. He's also been cheating on his income tax. I imagine the feds would be interested in that."

Bosley nodded. "I imagine that would." He took out his notebook and pen and handed them to Evans. "Okay, Mr. Evans, write your confession down here, and sign it. Mr. Lazenby and I will witness it."

"You'll put in a good word for me with the DA, right?"

"Why, yes, of course I will. Now, I'm also placing you under arrest for the murder of Gertrude Pope. You have the right to remain silent, if you give up that right, anything—"

"Yeah, yeah, I know. I'm relinquishing my right to remain silent, and I'll want a lawyer when I get to the jail. Right now, I just want to see that bastard, Harry Pope in handcuffs, too."

"You will, Mr. Evans," Bosley said. "As soon as you've signed that confession."

CHAPTER 27

It took Evans twenty minutes to write and sign his confession, another ten minutes for Bosley to locate and arrest Harry Pope, and a good thirty minutes, with the help of Ed, Ernesto, and Wilmot to keep the two men from ripping each other apart. They were finally locked in separate cabins awaiting the ferry with deputies from the sheriff station in Bar Harbor who would transport them to jail.

The ferry arrived five hours later, and Ed stood with Bosley and Hercules on the pier watching it sail away. Behind them, the rest of the team, the sergeant and his cadaver dog, the forensic specialist, and the backhoe operator, were checking their gear, making it ready to put on the next ferry to Bar Harbor.

"That was pretty ballsy, telling him that Pope had confessed and was trying to make a deal," Ed said. "What if he'd refused to fall for it?"

"Heck, Ed, he'd already fallen for that cockamamie story about the mud preserving DNA evidence, so I was pretty sure he'd buy that his accomplice was rolling over on him."

Ed's brows went up a quarter inch. "You mean that stuff about evidence wasn't right?"

"Frankly, I don't know. I doubt it, though. Even if it hadn't been submerged or buried, there's little likelihood we would've gotten any usable DNA off that scarf. He would've had to have bled on it, which he didn't."

"My, my, that was a neat bit of detective work, Trooper Bosley, no, I think pretty soon you'll be Detective Bosley."

"Heck, I couldn't have done it without your help, Ed."

"Oh, I think you would've done okay on your own. You're a quick study, and adaptable, and you've got good instincts. You're gonna make a fine detective. Your bosses don't need to know you had any help. You just have to make sure that Ms. Johnson doesn't say anything."

"Oh, she's cool, she won't say anything." In the distance another ferry was approaching. "Here comes our ferry. I have to get everyone settled. It's been a pleasure working with you, Ed. Anytime you're in Bar Harbor, look me up. I owe you a steak dinner."

He stuck out his hand.

Ed grasped.

"It was a pleasure, Nelson. And, I'll take you up on that steak."

CHAPTER 28

After all the excitement, Wilmot cancelled the day's training activity, and everyone turned in early.

But, the next morning, he was up at 6:00 am, blowing his whistle and rousting them out of their cabins. Ed, an early riser anyway, was dressed, but everyone else came out of their cabins in various stages of dress, none complete, hair rumpled, faces not made up, and expressions grumpy.

"Why are you getting us up so early?" asked Violet. "We're still getting over the trauma of past events."

Wilmot smiled his sunny smile at her and held up his clipboard. "The best way to get over trouble is not to pull your head in like a turtle, but to stretch your wings like an eagle," he said. "However, given events of the past few days, I called my brother last night, and we decided that if it's your wish, you can pack today and go home, and we'll refund your money."

Heads swiveled. Jaws dropped. Eyes went wide. To say that everyone was surprised at *this* turn of events would have been a gross understatement. Everyone was stunned, flummoxed, pole axed, and then, when it hit them what he'd said, saddened.

They looked at each other, each making eye contact with each of the others, and in that moment, something happened. Only Ed recognized it, and it almost brought tears to his eyes. He'd seen it before, when he was a young soldier. Fresh out of advanced training, on his first deployment into a combat zone. He was assigned with his van of specialized equipment to support an infantry unit on a special search and destroy mission to find and eliminate an enemy logistics base in the Central Highlands of Vietnam. They'd found the base all right, but the intelligence they'd been given had been flawed. Instead of being guarded by a battalion, it had been surrounded by a crack regiment of North Vietnamese regulars. In a relatively even battle, even considering the helicopter gunship support the Americans could call in, it quickly devolved into hand-to-hand, one bunker at a time fighting, with heavy casualties on both sides. In the end, though, American air support had tipped the scales, and the surviving North Vietnamese soldiers had been forced to retreat farther into the mountains. Ed had been in the thick of things, grabbing his M-16 and joining a squad assaulting a bunker, as his assigned job had ended as soon as they made contact with the enemy unit. Afterwards, preparing the dead and wounded to be taken by helicopter back to the firebase for onward shipment to Saigon, the wounded to the 97th Evacuation Hospital, and the dead to the Graves Registration Section where they would be prepared for shipment back home to their families, he saw the same shared look in their eyes. They'd gone through hell together, and that experience had formed an unbreakable bond. It could not be named or described and could only be appreciated by those who had earned it.

This little group had now become a 'band of brothers' so to speak, a close-knit group, closer even than blood kin, and they were reluctant to leave the place of their baptism. He'd seen that too. Soldiers who griped and bitched daily about being in 'Nam, and who just wanted to go back across the pond to the land of the big PX, after a battle would often put in a request for extension so they could stay with their buddies who still had time left on their tours.

He was tempted to say something, but was mindful of his bet with Wilmot, and besides, with Violet in the same situation, he didn't want to be the first to buckle.

It was Janet Evans who saved them. The shy, diffident woman who seemed afraid of her shadow, stepped forward, her shoulders square and her chin up, with a defiant expression on her face.

"I don't know about the others," she said. "But, I'd rather stay and finish out the week."

Violet moved up beside her and put her arms around the younger woman.

"Are you sure about this, dear? I mean, after all you've been through."

Lifting her face to look at Violet, she smiled broadly. "You mean, what we've all been through. I'm not going to lie, right now I feel free for the first time in a long, long time. I've endured hell for so many years I've lost count." She looked over at Ed. "Thanks to you and that policeman, I'm free. Do you know what that means? It means I can make my own decisions, and my decision is to stay here and enjoy the week Jason planned for us."

"Well," Violet said. "We can't let you stay alone. I suppose I could put up with a few more days."

Peter Pace and Daryl Drum joined the two women, Peter taking Janet's right hand, and Daryl, Violet's left.

"Count us in," Pace said. "Except for the unfortunate . . . incident, it's actually been quite fun, and I have to say, you guys are a great bunch."

Rose moved to stand next to Drum, and, of course, Ernesto stood beside her, leaving just Ed, and the Lakes.

Lilian Lake took her husband's hand. "What do you say, George? Should we stay the rest of the week?"

A beaming George Lake bobbed his head. "Indeedy," he said. "I'm in."

Wilmot looked at Ed.

"What about you, Ed? You staying, or should I call for the ferry to come back?"

"If there's one thing I dislike more than camping, it's boats, especially being the only passenger on a boat," Ed said.

"Is that a yes or no?"

"As long as you don't take it as a sign that I'm enjoying this, I suppose I'll stay."

Ed didn't miss the look Violet gave him, and he had some difficulty holding back the smile that threatened to break out on his face.

Books by this author

Al Pennyback mysteries
Color Me Dead
Memorial to the Dead
Deadline
Dead, White, and Blue
A Good Day to Die
The Day the Music Died
Die, Sinner
Deadly Intentions
Death by Design
Till Death Do Us Part
Deadly Dose
Dead Man's Cove
Dead Men Don't Answer
Deadly Paradise
Kiss of Death
Death in White Satin
Death and Taxis
Deadbeat
A Deadly Wind Blows
Death Wish
Deadly Vendetta
A Time to Kill, A Time to Die
Dead Ringer
Death of Innocence
Dead Reckoning
Murder on the Menu
Over My Dead Body
Bad Girls Don't Die
A Deal to Die For

Ed Lazenby mysteries
Butterfly Effect
Coriolis Effect

The Cat in the Hatbox
Negative Side Effects
Murder is as Easy as ABC
Body of Evidence

Buffalo Soldier series
Buffalo Soldier: Trial by Fire
Buffalo Soldier: Homecoming
Buffalo Soldier: Incident at Cactus Junction
Buffalo Soldier: Peacekeepers
Buffalo Soldier: Renegade
Buffalo Soldier: Escort Duty
Buffalo Soldier: Battle at Dead Man's Gulch
Buffalo Soldier: Yosemite
Buffalo Soldier: Comanchero
Buffalo Soldier: Range War
Buffalo Soldier: Mob Justice
Buffalo Soldier: Chasing Ghosts
Buffalo Soldier: The Piano
Buffalo Soldier: Family Feud
Buffalo Soldier: The Lost Expedition

Other fiction
Angel on His Shoulder
She's No Angel
Child of the Flame
Pip's Revenge
Wallace in Underland
Further Adventures of Wallace in Underland
Dead Letter and Other Tales
The White Dragons
The Dragon's Lair
Dragon Slayer
The Last Gunfighters
The Culling
Frontier Justice: Bass Reeves, Deputy U.S. Marshal
Angel on His Shoulder-Revised Edition

Battle at the Galactic Junkyard
Mountain Man
Devil's Lake
Vixen
Wagons West: Daniel's Journey
Wagons West: Trinity
Awakening
*Fatal Encounters: The Adventures of Bass
  Reeves, Deputy U.S. Marshal*
Chase the Sun
*The Marshal and the Madam: The Adventures of
  Bass Reeves, Deputy U.S. Marshal, Vol. 2*
*The Shaman's Curse: The Adventures of Bass
  Reeves, Deputy U.S. Marshal, Vol. 3*
*Renegade Roundup: The Adventures of Bass
  Reeves, Deputy U.S. Marshal, Vol. 4*

Nonfiction
*Things I Learned from My Grandmother About
  Leadership and Life*
*Taking Charge: Effective Leadership for the
  Twenty-first Century*
Grab the Brass ring
*African Places: A Photographic Journey
  Through Zimbabwe and southern Africa*
A Portrait of Africa
There's Always a Plan B
*In the Line of Fire: American Diplomats in
  the Trenches*
Advice for the Insecure Writer
Looking at Life Through My Lens
Ethical Dilemmas and the Practice of Diplomacy
Making America Grate Again
DC Street Art
Dead Letters and Other Tales: Revised edition
*Things I Learned From my Grandmother about
  Leadership and Life, Second Edition*
Feathers, Fur, and Flowers

Backyards and Byways

Children's books
The Yak and the Yeti
Samantha and the Bully
Molly Learns to Share
Where is Teddy?
Catie and Mister Hop-Hop
Tommy Learns to Count
Catie Goes to School

About the Author

Charles Ray has been writing fiction since his teens. He won a Sunday school magazine writing contest when he was thirteen and having his byline on a short story published in a national publication forever hooked him on writing. During his time in the army (1962-1982) he often moonlighted as a newspaper or magazine journalist and was the editorial cartoonist for the Spring Lake (NC) News, a weekly newspaper, during the 1970s. In addition to his writing, he was an artist/cartoonist and photographer for a number of publications, including Ebony, Eagle and Swan, and Essence, and had a monthly cartoon feature and did several covers for Buffalo, a now-defunct magazine that was dedicated to showcasing the contributions of African-Americans to the country's military history.

After retiring from the army, he joined the U.S. Foreign Service, and served as a diplomat in posts in Asia and Africa until his retirement in 2012. He has worked and traveled throughout the world (Antarctica is the only continent he hasn't visited), and now, as a full-time writer, continues to globetrot looking for interesting things to write about, draw, or take pictures of.

A native of Texas, he now calls Maryland home. For more on his writing and other projects, check one of the following Web sites:

http://charlesaray.blogspot.com
http://charlieray45.wordpress.com
http://www.twitter.com/charlieray45
http://www.facebook.com/charlieray45
http://www.flickr.com/photos/charlesray45/
http://www.viewbug.com/member/charlesray

You can also order some of my books through my author's website: http://charlesray-author.com/

Authors write to be read, and that can only happen when readers are made aware of the books available. Reviews are one way this happens. If you liked this book, please leave a review, even if only a few words, on Amazon or Goodreads.